The Polo Primer

The Polo Primer

A GUIDE FOR PLAYERS AND SPECTATORS

Steven D. Price

Charles Kauffman

THE STEPHEN GREENE PRESS
PELHAM BOOKS

Published by Penguin Books USA, Inc.

Viking Penguin Inc., 40 West 23rd Street, New York, New York 10010, U.S.A.

Penguin Books Ltd, 27 Wrights Lane, London W8 5TZ, England

Penguin Books Australia Ltd, Ringwood, Victoria, Australia

Penguin Books Canada Ltd, 2801 John Street, Markham, Ontario, Canada
  L3R 1B4

Penguin Books (N.Z.) Ltd, 182–190 Wairau Road, Auckland 10, New Zealand

Penguin Books Ltd, Registered Offices: Harmondsworth, Middlesex, England

First published in 1989 by The Stephen Greene Press
Published simultaneously in Canada
Distributed by Viking Penguin Inc.

10 9 8 7 6 5 4 3 2 1

Library of Congress Cataloging-in-Publication Data
Price, Steven D.
    The polo primer.
    1. Polo. I. Kauffman, Charles. II. Title.
GV1011.P75 1989   796.35′3   88-24353
ISBN 0-8289-0707-2

Designed by Deborah Schneider
Printed in the United States of America
Set in Kennerly Oldstyle by AccuComp Typographers
Produced by Unicorn Production Services, Inc.

Illustration used for chapter opener is from the Mayflower Mills trademark, from the book *Trademarks of the 20's and 30's* by Eric Baker and Tyler Blik (San Francisco: Chronicle Books).

To Eduardo Moore
"How awesome a man on horseback
can seem to a man on foot."

Contents

Introduction

Polo is charging into the twenty-first century at a full gallop. From the aristocratic venues of Europe to balmy social settings in Palm Beach and Saratoga, from the palaces of Brunei to the palm-ringed polo fields of Hawaii, polo is on the crest of a great wave of enthusiasm. Mallets are being swung in colleges, huge arenas, and exquisite clubs by a continuous new stream of devotees, men and women. Private polo fields are replacing the status of "your own tennis court." With more clubs, teams, and players than ever before, it is time to examine the reasons for polo's historic and continuing attraction.

Winston Churchill said that a polo handicap is the best letter of introduction in the world. Entering the world of polo, you join the "aristocracy of physical force." Although called "the sport of kings and the King of Sports," it is seen correctly by Nelson Aldrich as "the sport of warriors, the guards of power" who defend and enable kings to conquer and rule. When Francisco Dorignac stated recently, "we Argentines are the best and we cannot make allowances," he recalled an ancient battle cry.

Polo is too serious to be a sport and too frivolous to be a profession. It becomes obsessive and, in some cases, takes over people's lives. It is a civilized man's war. Polo is not a gentle game. The ancient Persians said, "may the heads of your enemies be your polo balls." While he may try to persuade himself that it is just a hobby, a serious player has to win.

"Polo should be played with hot blood and a cool head," says ten-goal rated premier player, Gonzalo Pieres. To win, an athlete must possess certain mental skills: concentration, positive thinking, the ability to control attitude and energy, the ability to manage pressure, continuous motivation, and visualization. The few top players usually have a well-developed sense of anticipation, and quickness of thought and action. In the realm of the great players, Juan Carlos Harriot said he preferred a player with *garra*, a consuming desire to win, over one with excellent skills, horses, and conditioning.

Polo is more than the "rodeo of the rich." It deals with courage and pushing beyond the barrier of dread. One player laughingly speaks of having his "daily dose of fear." Polo is elusive. Adam Lindemann says, "You always need something more. You want a better horse, a better field, a better team. In the end, polo will always escape you."

Physically, there is no other team contact sport that you can play indefinitely. The horse is your legs, and you can play as long as you are athletic enough to stay on.

Borne on the back of the horse, man's oldest craft of voyage, playing his oldest recorded ball game, lovers of polo share what Jerzy Kosinski describes in *Passion Play* as "the seduction of a perfect shot . . . eye and thought strained to the target . . . striking faultlessly the center of the ball."

Like the armorers of old, the 113-year history of H. KAUFFMAN & SONS SADDLERY COMPANY is inextricably linked to polo. Throughout our history, such greats as Tommy Hitchcock, Jock Whitney, Pete Bostwick, Cecil Smith, Mike Phipps, Horacio Heguey, Eduardo Moore, Christian LaPrida, the three brothers Gonzalo, Paul, and Alfonso Pieres, Memo Gracida, Antonio Herrera, and players from over forty nations have asked us to provide their equipment. Polo is played off the field as well as on, and players demand style, performance, and durability—nothing less than the best. It is our hope that this book will increase your interest, understanding, and participation in man's best game.

CHARLES F. KAUFFMAN
H. Kauffman & Sons Saddlery Company
New York City

STEVEN D. PRICE
New York City
December 1988

Polo—An Overview

—The sport of polo is often referred to as "hockey on horseback." As in hockey, the object of polo is to score more goals than the opposing team. A goal, which is worth one point, is scored when the ball passes between the opponent's goalposts, whether by a player's mallet, or even by the player's horse, or by an opponent.

—The ball most often used in outdoor play is made of high-impact plastic or wood, and weighs four ounces. It is capable of reaching speeds up to 100 miles an hour.

—A regulation-size outdoor polo field measures 300 yards long by 160 yards wide. This 10-acre area is the equivalent of nine football fields. Goalposts at each of the far ends are spaced 8 yards apart. Low sideboards, approximately 10 inches high, run the lengths of the field's two long sides.

—An outdoor polo match consists of 6 chukkers, or periods. There are 5-minute rest periods between chukkers, with a longer break between the midpoint third and fourth chukkers. Each chukker lasts 7 minutes, plus up to 30 seconds of overtime. The overtime portion will end before the 30 seconds have elapsed in the event that the ball hits against the sideboards or goes out of bounds, or when the referee signals a goal or a penalty. There is no overtime portion of the sixth, or final chukker, unless the score is tied. In that case, a "sudden death" seventh chukker will last until a goal is scored.

Time is stopped when a referee calls a foul or when a player is seriously injured. Time is not stopped when a player voluntarily leaves the field to change mallets or ponies.

Teams switch goals (ends of the field) at the end of each chukker.

—There are two teams of four players each in outdoor polo. Members of each team wear distinctively colored shirts for identification.

Each player is assigned a position. The Number One player, who ranges closest to the opposing team's goal, is basically responsible for receiving passes and scoring goals. The Number Two player, who has a similar function, plays slightly behind this spearhead position. The role of the Number Three is, whenever possible, to turn the tide of play and recapture the offense when the other team has possession of the ball. The primary role of the Number Four, or Back, is that of a goalie.

Given the fast and fluid nature of the flow of a game, players may be momentarily out of position, but they will return to their relative positions as soon as warranted.

—In arena, or indoor polo, the dimensions of individual riding halls or arenas determine the size of the playing area, although 300 feet by 150 feet is considered ideal. Goals, which are set at the midpoint of the opposite ends of the arena, measure 10 feet wide by 12 feet high.

An indoor team consists of three players: a Number One, a Number Two, and a Number Three. The game is divided into 4 periods of 7 minutes each. The ball, made of leather with an inflatable rubber bladder, or of inflatable plastic, measures 4½ inches in diameter and weighs approximately 8 ounces. An inflatable leather ball is required for tournament play.

—Player equipment for both outdoor and arena polo includes high-heeled English- or Western-style polo boots, white breeches, a polo shirt, and a protective helmet. Knee guards afford protection for that vulnerable area, while gloves provide a more secure grip on the reins and mallet. Players usually carry a long, thin whip and wear spurs of either the blunt or rounded-rowel variety.

—The mallet, or stick, ranges in length from 48 to 54 inches, depending on the player's preference. The shaft is made of flexible bamboo (graphite and other man-made shafts are gaining in popularity among some players). The cigar-shaped head can be bamboo, maple, tipa (a tree native to Argentina), or any other hardwood. The mallet is *always* carried in the player's right hand (using one's left hand is against the rules), and the player strikes the ball with the long side of the mallet head, not the end. In the event that a mallet snaps or is otherwise damaged, the player will hurry to the sideline for a replacement.

—Horses used in polo are traditionally referred to as ponies (a reminder of the sport's early days when there was a size limitation on mounts). Despite the word, there is now no restriction on an animal's size, although most stand between 15 and 16 hands high (a "hand" equals 4 inches, with measurement taken from the withers, roughly in front of the saddle, to the ground). The majority of polo ponies are thoroughbreds; many have been specially bred for the sport, while others have had careers as race horses. Because of the pace and the physical demands of the sport, tournament players usually use a fresh pony for each chukker. In low-goal games, a pony usually plays 2 chukkers with a rest between the periods it plays.

A pony's tack includes an English-style saddle (with the addition of a breastplate across the animal's chest to keep the saddle from slipping backwards). The bridle, which often includes draw reins, may contain any of a variety of bits. A martingale, a strap that runs between the horse's forelegs from the girth to the bridle, keeps the animal's head from flying up into the rider's face. The pony's lower legs are wrapped with protective wrappings, while a tail wrap prevents the long hair from getting tangled in the player's mallet.

A pony's training involves learning to understand and obey the rider's cues. A rider's leg pressure is a signal to move forward, while hand pressure (via the reins and bit) is the cue to stop. A pony is also taught to neck-rein, or turn at the pressure of the reins against its neck. A difficult yet essential maneuver is the 180-degree turn on the haunches that the pony must be taught to perform at the gallop as well as the halt.

In order to remain in balance at the gallop, the pony must be on the correct lead (a horse is on the left or right lead depending on which fore- and hind-leg combination leads, or strikes the ground first in the sequence of footfalls at the canter or gallop). Therefore, polo ponies are taught flying changes, to switch leads without breaking stride, first at the trainer's instructions and, with time and training, automatically, without any cue from the rider.

—Two mounted umpires monitor an outdoor match; arena polo has only one. They start and halt play, as well as call fouls in the event of any infractions of the rules. If they cannot agree on whether a foul has been committed, they consult with a third official, the referee, who watches the game from the grandstand.

—Play begins with a throw-in at the start of each chukker, and after goals and successful penalty shots. As the two teams line up at midfield, an umpire tosses the ball onto the ground between them.

—The four basic mallet strokes are the near- (or right-side) forehand and backhand, and the off- (left-side) forehand and backhand. There are also neck shots, in which a player strokes the ball by reaching under his pony's neck, and tail shots, by which the ball is stroked behind the horse's tail.

—The most important "rule of the road" is honoring the line of the ball, an imaginary line indicating the path in which an opponent has hit the ball. A defensive player who crosses the line dangerously close in front of the player who "has the line" has committed a foul.

—Riding off, the most important defensive maneuver, involves attempting to bump or push an opponent away from the ball by causing one's pony to bump against the opponent's pony. Any collision at an angle of more than 45 degrees, however, is a foul.

—Another defensive technique is to prevent an opponent from stroking the ball by hooking, or blocking, his mallet with the defensive player's own stick. This may be done only on the same side of the opponent's pony that the player is attempting to strike the ball ("cross hooking" constitutes a foul, as does "high hooking" above the horse's rump).

—Other fouls include reaching under or in front of an opponent's pony, and abusing one's own pony.

—Fouls result in penalties, which are based on the severity of the infraction of the rules. Penalties range from automatic goals to shots from various distances against undefended or defended goals.

—A match traditionally concludes with players congratulating members of the opposing team as soon as the game is over.

The Polo Primer

One

Polo—Past and Present

The sport of polo, reputed to be the most ancient of mounted sports, originated in Asia. The earliest references are found in writings dating from the reigns of Alexander the Great and Darius of Persia more than 2500 years ago, including an account of a match played between the Persians and the Turkomans.

As Alexander and other military leaders moved across Asia, they introduced the sport to lands they visited and conquered. Horsemen of all cultures saw the game not only as exciting recreation, but as an important way to hone their military skills. Mongolian tribesmen brought the game to China and Japan. High in the Himalayas, Tibetan horsemen called the sport *pulu*, their word for a type of willow root from which they carved the ball used in the game (and from which the word "polo" is derived).

Muslim and Chinese invaders introduced the sport into northern India. British cavalrymen stationed there in the nineteenth century learned the game from native troops and from English plantation owners who had already settled in India. Silchar, the capital of the Cachar district near the Burmese border, is considered the birthplace of Anglo-Indian polo. The Silchar Club, the oldest polo club in the world, was founded in 1859, and the rules of the game drawn up there are the foundation of the game as it is played today. The number of players on a side was reduced from nine to seven, and then to the present-day four. Another enduring Indian influence is the word chukker, a Hindu word for each period of play.

Polo was introduced into England in 1869 by returning cavalry officers. The Hurlingham Club became the seat of British polo, codifying the rules of English polo in 1875. Among the regulations was a restriction on the size of the players' mounts; only ponies standing 14 hands or smaller (56 inches, measured from the withers to the ground) were permitted.

Among the spectators at the club that year was a visitor from America, James Gordon Bennett, the publisher of the New York *Herald*. Captivated by the lightning action and bold horsemanship, he returned to the United States in 1876 with mallets, balls, and an evangelical zeal for polo. Mounting his friends on cow ponies that he had brought from the West, Bennett taught them the sport's fundamentals, and unwilling to wait until better weather, he staged America's first polo match in a New York City indoor riding arena during the winter of 1876–7.

The first outdoor game was held in May at Jerome Park, a Bronx racetrack (continuing the Anglo-American connection, the track was named after Winston Churchill's maternal grandfather). Another nearby site was called the Polo Grounds, subsequently and better known as the home field of the pre-San Francisco Giants baseball team. Other clubs were formed, and soon polo became a favorite pastime of America's sporting gentry.

Gear, rules, and play during this early era of polo could best be described as rudimentary. Players who lacked equipment imported from England improvised by extending the handles of croquet mallets. Teams had five players on a side, and scrimmage-like "every man for himself" play went on until a goal was scored. As the sport developed, however, limits were set with regard to time of play; there were 4 quarters of 20 minutes each, with 5-minute rest periods between them.

The first international polo match took place in 1886. Teams from Britain and the United States competed in Rye, New York, for the Westchester Cup (Great Britain won). Nine matches in all were played over the years for that trophy, the last in 1936.

Polo clubs proliferated. Thanks to Bennett's influence and proximity, New York City had several. On Long Island were the prestigious Meadow Brook and Rockaway hunting clubs, while others along the Eastern seaboard were to be found in Saratoga, Boston, Newport, and Aiken in South Carolina's hunt country.

With so many clubs eager to play against each other, but with no standard rules, the United States Polo Association was formed in 1890. Under the leadership of H. L. Herbert, the association made uniform rules and established the system of handicapping, or rating, players according to their skills. Each player received an annually revised rating between zero (the lowest) and ten (for the most proficient). In an effort to assure an equality of outcome, the numerical ratings of all the players on each of both teams were totalled, with any difference being awarded at the start of the match as goals for the team with the lower total.

The early twentieth century saw the expansion of polo in proportions that even James Gordon Bennett might not have envisioned. Wealthy sportsmen in California became as avid players as their East Coast counterparts. At the urging of General John J. Pershing, the U.S. Army furnished horses and equipment to military bases, where

officers advanced their careers as well as their equestrian skills by outstanding and bold play. Through colleges' ROTC programs, the sport became a part of undergraduate life on many campuses. Riding academies throughout the country included indoor polo as part of their programs; goalposts were painted on the arenas' end walls, and an inflatable rubber ball was used.

Playing techniques developed during this period, too. Rather than the free-for-all melees that had marked American polo's formative years, teamwork strategies emphasized field position and the passing game. Western cow ponies were bred to Thoroughbreds to develop a strain of American polo pony.

America's golden age of polo spanned the decades between World Wars One and Two. Among the legendary players of this era were Cecil Smith (rated at ten goals for an unprecedented 25 years), Tommy Hitchcock, Jr. (a ten-goal rated player for 18 years), Devereaux Milburn, Eric Pedley, and George "Pete" Bostwick. Top-flight amateurs included Raymond and Winston Guest, Sonny Whitney, John Hay Whitney, Mike Phipps, and W. Averell Harriman. American squads, composed of these and other outstanding players, competed against each other in matches that attracted tens of thousands of spectators. At home and abroad, American squads represented their country in matches against the best of Great Britain and, among other countries, Argentina, where polo became something of a national mania. Argentina became the sport's most formidable international force beginning in the mid-1930s and continues to be so today.

Increasing numbers of people who had the requisite time and wherewithal discovered the thrill of playing polo. More than eighty clubs throughout the United States were among host facilities for the thousands of veteran and novice players. Hollywood became a center, and the media avidly covered such luminary moguls and stars as Walt Disney, Darryl Zanuck, Louis B. Mayer, Clark Gable, Spencer Tracy, and Will Rogers.

Polo also had an impact on this pre-Ralph Lauren era's fashions. A generation of college coeds and others wore camel's-hair "polo" coats and Brooks Brothers button-down collar shirts (the buttons prevented shirt lapels from flapping in a player's face).

Polo experienced an ebb during and following World War Two. The mechanization of the military refocused the Army's attention away from horses and horsemanship, while the war itself created a shortage of players and a shortage of time to train ponies. Some polo complexes fell victim to postwar residential and commercial land development, and spiraling expenses of maintaining a string of ponies deterred many sportsmen who might otherwise have engaged in the sport. Public interest also waned as the social allure of attending or following matches and tournaments gave way to other spectator and media activities.

That is not to say, however, that there was no polo at all. The Oak Brook Polo Club outside Chicago became a center for tournament play, highlighted by the Open Championships, American polo's World Series. The Gulfstream Polo Club in Florida was the vanguard of activity in that state.

The 1960s saw a turn of the tide. From Florida's Royal Palm in Boca Raton, to Willow Bend in Houston and Santa Barbara in California, the sport regained its pre-war momentum. The Cup of the Americas tournament between the U.S. and Argentina was resumed in 1966, while the four-year Coronation Cup series between the U.S. and Great Britain took place between 1971 and 1974.

The year 1976 marked not only American polo's centennial but the inauguration of corporate sponsorship. Under the aegis of its chairman, William Ylversaker, the Gould Corporation participated in that year's World Championship through $25,000 in prize money and the Gould World Cup trophy. In subsequent years, hundreds of commercial interests discovered the value of corporate advertising and promotional involvement in polo, until now few major tournaments are without such support. Among those sponsors with a substantial interest in polo are Rolex, Glenlivet, Abercrombie & Kent, Cadillac, and Pimms Cup. Another, Piaget, was the sponsor of the Piaget World Cup, the first tournament in this country to offer $100,000 in prize money.

The 1970s also witnessed a proliferation of polo locations, including West Palm Beach's Palm Beach Polo and Country Club, a large residential and sports complex devoted to the sport. Celebrity tournaments and exhibitions, there and elsewhere, harken back to the era when Hollywood stars and magnates played; such movie and television luminaries as Alex Cord, William Devane, and Stephanie Powers are avid players.

Television has also discovered the sport, with network and cable coverage of important matches and tournaments introducing polo to

millions of viewers. Television commercials and magazine print adver-
tisements have taken advantage of polo's image to associate products
and services with the sport.

Since the growth of arena polo has kept pace with its outdoor
cousin, there are now scores of opportunities for indoor play, an especially welcome alternative where hard winters and inclement weather
make fields unplayable, as well as where outdoor space limitation
is a factor.

Polo today is a happy beneficiary of the widespread growth of interest in horse sports. Among those who have discovered the excitement
and satisfaction of playing polo are riders who started their equestrian
careers in the show ring or dressage arena. Indeed, many riders who
no longer have the time or interest in showing have now swapped
their hunt caps for polo helmets (the team aspect of the sport seems
to be an especially appealing factor in their change).

Once an all-male bastion, polo now counts women among its most
enthusiastic participants. They play an integral part in polo on the
interscholastic level, while practice and play on the club level includes
mixed squads and teams, as well as all-female teams and leagues.

Nor is age a restrictive factor—people can begin at the "Little
League" level and play all the way up to their sixties and beyond
(one legendary club player in the Northeast continued well into his
seventies—what he lacked in physical strength was more than com-
pensated for by his experience and "field generalship").

Among polo's active participants are people who never hold a mallet. Whether they choose to bypass the physical demands placed
on players or simply because they enjoy the role of officiating, the
referees and umpires are always in demand as essential elements of
games and matches at all levels of play.

A vital aspect of the sport today is the widespread effort to ac-
quaint the public with polo (as well as to shed its "elitist" image).
Many clubs have some sort of Introduction to Polo program that
supplies novices with ponies, equipment, and first-rate basic instruction. Equally important and active are intercollegiate and interscholastic organizations, which provide ample opportunities for the next
generation of polo participants and spectators. In neither case is own-
ing a horse a requirement. Polo clinics and vacations at resorts in
the Americas and elsewhere provide a "busman's holiday" for players
at all levels, as well as a way for prospective players to learn the game.

Indoor action during a women's tournament held at the Los Angeles Equestrian Center, the largest arena polo facility in the United States. (Ross A. Benson)

The roster of polo clubs, interscholastic and intercollegiate groups, and clinic opportunities listed in Chapter Nine is a comprehensive guide to places where interested readers can find out more about entering the world of polo.

Two

Equipment

The Mallet

A mallet, or stick, is as important to a polo player as a bat is for a baseball player or a racquet for a tennis player. Just as there is no universally right-size bat or racquet, so novice polo players will have to learn what length, weight, degree of shaft "whippiness," and mallet-head shape are most appropriate.

A mallet is composed of a head, a shaft, a handle, and a wrist strap.

Mallet heads are made of such hardwoods as bamboo, maple, and tipa (a tree native to Argentina). Bamboo is a favorite because of its resistance to splitting or splintering. Maple permits hitting a greater distance, although it lacks bamboo's ability to absorb the shock of

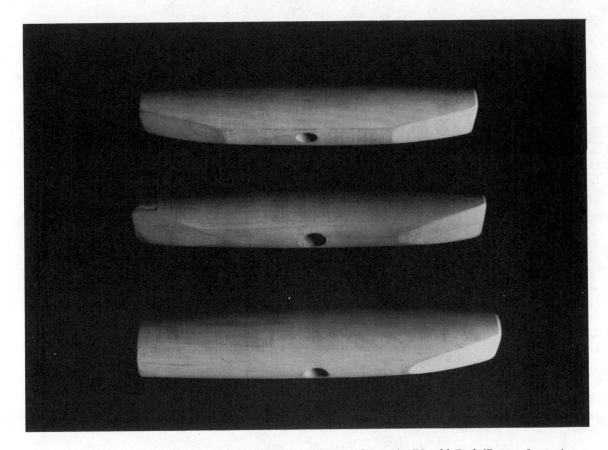

Mallet head shapes: skene (top), R.N.P.A. (middle), and cigar (bottom). (Harold Roth/Equine Images)

the impact. The rear end of the head is called the "heel," and the front end is called the "toe."

Mallet heads weigh from 6 to 8 ounces, and measure approximately 9 inches long and from 1½ to 2 inches in diameter. They come in four distinctive shapes.

Both ends of the **cigar** head taper down to a one-inch end, giving the head its cigar shape and name. The bulk of the weight is in the center where the head strikes the ball (the so-called "sweet spot"), and the shape permits maximum driving power.

The **skene** is another widely used model. Designed by and named for a player named Bob Skene, it has a flat bottom but both ends are tapered at the same angle.

More specialized is the **clip cigar**, which has one end cut on the bias to a flat taper. The two ends thus offer a choice of different striking surfaces; tapered ends are said to create greater loft, while rounded ends produce greater drive.

The **RNPA** (the initials stand for Royal Naval Polo Association) is yet another variation of the cigar head. Its midsection is rounded, but its ends are tapered flat.

Like the choice of baseball bats and tennis racquets, personal preference and abilities determine the choice of a mallet head's shape and weight. Most beginners start out with a lightweight cigar head, which offers the greatest amount of hitting surface and is the easiest to wield.

Experienced players who opt for heavier heads, which facilitate "long ball" hitting, intentionally sacrifice some degree of balance, since manufacturers assemble mallets so the weight of the head relates to the stiffness of the shaft: the heavier the head, the stiffer the shaft.

The shaft of most mallets is made of bamboo cane, its base wrapped above the head with cord to help protect the stick from snapping. The more joints in the cane, the stronger and more flexible the wood. A shaft's flexibility is measured in terms of stiffness (more flexible shafts are called "whippy"), and sticks come in three degrees: medium stiff, stiff, and extra stiff. The type of shaft flexibility a player uses depends on personal preference, although medium stiff is the most popular.

Fiberglass and graphite are modern alternatives to wooden shafts, with the advantage that they are virtually unbreakable. However, bamboo absorbs the shock of impact better than the man-made materials do, and is thus less likely to lead to a player's developing the polo equivalent of a "tennis elbow."

The rubberized handle of a mallet can be one of three shapes. The **Parada**, or pistol grip, has a flat base on its top and a contoured underside; the bulge separates the holder's index finger from the other fingers. The Parada is popular with beginners and other players who hold their mallets in a finger grip.

The **Lloyd** grip is flat on both sides, its tapered shape permitting a hand to slide up or down until the most comfortable handhold is found. Similar to the Lloyd, the **rugby** grip is slightly flatter.

The wrist strap, or sling, is simply a length of ¾-inch cotton webbing fastened to the end of the mallet, which a player wraps around his wrist as a safety belt to keep the mallet securely in his hand.

CHOOSING THE RIGHT MALLET

Polo mallets come in different lengths, their overall lengths measured in inches. The most common lengths range between 49 and 53 inches. Although as a novice player, you won't know which length is best for you until you try a variety of sticks, several general principles will be useful.

It is obvious that a stick must be long enough for you to make contact with the ball. The correct length will therefore depend on your size and the size of the pony on which you are mounted, but equally important, you must be able to stroke the ball comfortably and naturally. These factors involve determining your natural swing, which can be done only from the back of a pony or a wooden practice horse, and with the assistance of your coach or another experienced player.

If you are of average height (anywhere from 5 feet 7 inches to 5 feet 10 inches) and you are on an average-sized pony (15 to 15½ hands), a 51 inch mallet is the one your coach will probably recommend you use at first. If during the course of practicing or play, you find or are told that you are dropping your shoulder (as if to reach down for the ball), you will need a longer stick. On the other hand, raising your shoulder is an indication that a shorter length will be needed.

Mallets weigh slightly more than one pound. Since the weight of the head constitutes almost half of the total weight, as a beginning player you may want to start with one that is somewhat on the lighter end of the scale, until your wrist and arm become stronger with exercise. Similarly, as your body becomes more supple, you may find yourself gravitating toward a stick with a shorter shaft.

PROPER CARE OF MALLETS

—Store your mallets by hanging them by their straps, never by their heads.

—Heat softens bamboo and dries out the wood's natural resiliency. Keep mallets out of direct sunlight for prolonged periods of time, and never store them near radiator heat.

—Mallet heads that have become chipped should be repainted to prevent moisture from rotting the wood (moisture-soaked wood will also produce a heavier head).

The Helmet

No one should ever sit on a horse, much less play a contact sport like polo, without wearing a protective hard hat. A polo helmet has been specifically designed to withstand the impact of a ball or mallet, as well as to offer protection to the wearer's head in case of a fall. It is made of crush-proof Royalite lined with foam rubber padding and a padded leather sweatband, and it includes a securely attached chin strap. Many players choose a helmet that has a metal face guard, which protects the face without impairing the wearer's vision.

Any helmet that does not fit properly offers less than maximum protection, while headgear that has cracked or a strap that has loosened or frayed should be discarded and professionally replaced.

Footwear and Leg Wear

Polo boots, which combine the support and protection found in both English- and Western-style boots, are traditionally made of brown tooled leather. Like English boots, they are cut high to protect the rider's legs up to the knee. Their high underslung Western heels are designed to keep the wearer's feet from slipping through the stirrups.

The zipper-front style permits ease in putting them on and taking them off.

Breeches are traditionally and appropriately worn with high boots. Their seat and legs should fit snugly to eliminate chafing and saddle sores; stretch fabrics are used for that reason. Although tournament play calls for white, breeches of any color would be acceptable for practicing or scrimmaging.

An alternative to boots and breeches, especially for practice and scrimmaging, are chaps and low boots. Polo, or schooling, chaps are made of sturdy suede leather. They have industrial-strength zippers that run down the length of the leggings and zip over jeans or any other snug-fitting pants.

Any type of riding shoe or low boot, especially laced paddock boots or strapped or zipped jodphur boots, goes with chaps. The important thing to remember is that the footwear must have well-defined heels to keep feet from slipping through the stirrups.

Whatever footwear you choose, leather products will last longer if you clean them after every use. Wipe off mud and dirt with a damp sponge. A periodic application of a leather dressing will keep the boots from drying and cracking. Very wet leather should be allowed to dry before being treated with the dressing, and in all cases, using boot trees will help maintain the shape of footwear.

Other Apparel and Accessories

A polo shirt gets its name from the sport, and a loose, comfortably fitting placket-neck polo shirt is more than appropriate for all kinds of polo activity. It can be topped in cooler weather with a sweatshirt, or a cotton turtleneck can be worn underneath.

Another polo-named item is the polo belt, a wide canvas or wool belt with built-in stays that provide support for stresses and strains to abdominal and lower back muscles. Not all players wear this belt, but if you do, make sure it fits snugly.

Knee guards are made of supple leather over foam rubber or thick wool padding. They strap onto the knees and provide protection against fast-flying balls, mallets, and the impact of an opponent's pony during a ride-off.

Riding gloves help the player's hands get a better grip on both

Outfitted for tournament play, the player wears a helmet, white breeches, and polo boots. His short-sleeved shirt is in his team's colors. Like most players, he wears spurs and gloves. Note that the helmet's chin strap is securely in place. It cannot be overemphasized that no one should ride—whether playing or practicing—without wearing regulation safety headgear. (Harold Roth/Equine Images)

the reins and the mallet. They are especially useful in combatting perspiration in warm weather.

Most experienced players routinely wear spurs and carry a whip. Spurs are either the English-style blunt "Prince of Wales" model, or with smooth (called coin) rowels. The polo whip, measuring 39 inches, has a mushroom head and a leather wrist loop, both intended to keep the stick from slipping out of the player's left hand.

Three

The Polo Pony

It is often said that the pony accounts for 80 percent of any player's success, for without a well-trained, responsive, and durable mount, even the best player will be at a disadvantage.

Unlike the kinds of horses used in some other equestrian sports, there is no requirement that a polo pony be a specific breed. Horses with all or some Thoroughbred blood are especially valued for their speed, but you will also see Quarter Horses, Arabians, and Morgans, such "color" breeds as Appaloosas, Palominos, and Pintos, and cross-breeds and "grades" (horses of no discernable breeding).

Within this wide range, certain characteristics mark individual horses as the polo pony type, the kind that will be most suited to take part in the sport.

Although there are no size limits, the ideal pony will stand between 15 and 15.2 hands high (approximately 6 feet tall measured at the withers). Horses that are much shorter or taller will be out of propor-tion to the size of the average player, which will make hitting the ball more difficult than it should be.

There are also no age restrictions, and many horses well into their twenties are still capable of teaching beginning players and taking part in slow-paced practice sessions and games.

Physical ability is a prerequisite. Polo ponies must be able to gallop fast and easily. They must also be able to stop "on a dime," and then wheel up to a 180-degree turn and accelerate back to the gal-lop in the shortest possible time, as well as execute flying changes of lead. Therefore, any animal that has chronic wind or leg ailments will not be a useful mount. Stamina is an allied consideration; a pony that tires easily will be not only useless, but a danger to others.

Like successful athletes in other sports, ideal polo ponies show desire and courage, or in other words, "heart." They have no reluc-tance to do anything asked of them—in fact, these animals seem to enjoy the galloping and close contact.

"Polo sense" is another innate quality. It is an intelligence (although developed by experience) that makes such ponies seem to have minds of their own, an ability to anticipate the flow of play, such as when to check or which way to turn. No matter what its age, a pony so blessed will never lose this ability, and if you are lucky enough to be assigned such an animal as your first pony, you will be well-mounted indeed.

Polo Tack

Although your introduction to the tack worn by polo ponies will come firsthand from the equipment on the animal on which you have your first lessons, you should be aware of the variety, as well as the constants, of such gear.

The **polo saddle** is a type of all-purpose English saddle. Its wide and deep seat provides support and security, while its wide cantle allows ease of movement.

Fittings will include extra-strong red buffalo or rawhide stirrup leathers, and wide (5 inch to 5½ inch) heavy stainless steel stirrups with nonslip rubber treads. Many players prefer to keep the saddle in place by means of a three-ply Balding, or a shaped anti-chafing leather girth without elastic ends; the three sections lie flat under the horse's belly and are less likely to slip than other types of girths. In the same vein, many players also use an overgirth for extra security.

A sheepskin or synthetic fleece saddle pad reduces the chance of the saddle chafing and pinching. Many players, however, use only a saddle blanket (often a decorated "Navajo") between the saddle and the horse's back.

A polo standing martingale, a wide reinforced heavy leather strap that runs between the horse's forelegs from the girth to the noseband, prevents the animal from tossing or raising its head.

Polo saddles are also secured with the help of a breastplate, a wide leather strap that passes across the horse's chest. The ends of the strap are attached to rings on either side of the front of the saddle, and the strap itself held in place with another length of leather over the horse's withers.

Thick, wide fleece leg bandages wrapped and then taped around the pony's lower legs are less for decoration than for support and protection. The pony's tail will be tied up or taped to keep it from becoming entangled in its rider's mallet or the ball.

BITS

In order to understand the action of various bits worn by polo ponies, it is helpful to know that there are seven areas where a bit can exert pressure. They are: the tongue, the bars (the space in the horse's mouth between the incisor teeth and the molars), the roof of the mouth, the lips, the chin (also called the curb groove), the nose, and the poll (the sensitive portion of the horse's head behind the ears).

The **snaffle**, which acts on the bars, the tongue, and the lips, causes a horse to raise its head. Few polo ponies are ridden in only a snaffle, but the bit is often combined with a **curb** bit. The curb acts on five areas: the bars, the tongue, the roof of the mouth (via the rounded port on the top of the bit), the curb groove (by means of the strap or chain that extends around the back of the horse's jaw), and the poll (via the bridle itself). A curb bit encourages a horse

This pony is wearing a gag snaffle bit, with a set of draw reins passing through the snaffle rings. A breastplate helps to hold the saddle in place. Leg and tail wraps complete the pony's "outfit." (Harold Roth/Equine Images)

to arch its neck and tuck its chin against its chest, producing more responsive halts than a snaffle can.

The **double bridle**, or Weymouth, and the **pelham**, literally combine curb and snaffle bits. The double bridle is simply two bits, one curb and one snaffle (here called the bradoon), while the more popular pelham is an all-in-one device. In both cases, there are two sets of reins, one for the curb and another for the snaffle, which the rider operates in concert or with different amounts of pressure. The snaffle reins are slightly wider than the ones for the curb. Novice polo players often find the two sets of reins a literal handful, but more experienced riders welcome the added control that the double bridle or pelham gives. The **gag**, or gag snaffle, a popular bit in polo, also combines the effect of a snaffle and a curb bit. Its cheekpieces pass through holes in the bit, and as the reins pull back, the bit slides upward. The effect is thus not only against the lips and bars of the horse's mouth, but against the poll (simultaneously exerting a raising and lowering effect).

Within these categories are dozens of specialized types of bits; within the snaffle and gag snaffle group, for example, are jointed, twisted, thick, thin, double, and combinations thereof. Materials include hard rubber, steel, and copper. Each bit shape, size, and material has its specific effect, and which type or combination of bits will be most effective on a particular polo pony depends on such factors as the animal's responsiveness, disposition, and amount of training, as well as the player's ability and personal preference.

REINS

Acting somewhat like a running martingale, **draw reins** are a very popular although sophisticated method of control. One end of the pair of reins attaches to the girth, with the other end passing through the rings of the horse's bit, ending in the rider's hands. Draw reins intensify the bit's action, and they are especially useful for effecting quick stops and turns.

The type of bit or bits worn by your pony will, to a large measure, determine the type of reins that your pony's bridle will require. Nevertheless, the action and physical stress of the game demand strong yet supple leather, and care must be taken to insure that all items (not just reins) be maintained in excellent condition. Common-sense safety considerations require that worn leather and frayed or loose buckles and stitching need to be immediately replaced (and then, if possible, professionally repaired for future use). If this advice seems abstract, just imagine having a rein or stirrup break while you're galloping after a ball or when an opponent tries to ride you off the line, and you'll understand exactly.

Polo Horsemanship

Although this guide is not intended as a how-to-ride manual, a brief discussion of certain basic techniques will emphasize their importance.

Foot position: fundamental to security in the saddle, especially at times when almost all your weight will be on one foot, is not losing your stirrups. The correct position for your feet is "well home," or thrust through the stirrups so that the threads of the irons are under your arches, not on the balls of your feet (as you may have been taught when you learned to ride). This position also encourages your body to pivot at your waist, which will be of great importance when you are stroking the ball.

Riding left-handed: people who start out learning to ride hold a rein in each hand. When you start your polo training, however, you will need to become adept at controlling your pony by means of both reins held in your left hand. If you are unaccustomed to riding this way, practice shifting the reins, then riding forward and turning in this fashion. Work on making a smooth shift, keeping equal tension on your pony's mouth.

Although you will carry a mallet in your right hand, you will not give up using your right hand on the reins. Riding with both hands provides greater control of a pony, and when players are not stroking the ball (some 95 percent of the time), they keep the last two fingers of their right hand on the right rein. Picking up and dropping the rein with those fingers is an exercise to practice.

Neck-reining: a horse that is ridden one-handed is asked to turn by means of a technique called neck-reining. Here, the horse responds to pressure of the rein on its neck, on the side away from the direction in which the horse will turn. To turn left, for example, you would draw your hand directly to the left; pressure from the right rein against its neck encourages your horse to swing its head, neck, and forequarters to the left. The left rein plays no part in this maneuver, except as its tension is correspondingly relaxed.

Neck-reining moves only the horse's forequarters, so you will need to reinforce your hand with leg pressure. As you draw your hand to the left for a left-hand turn, increase the pressure of your right leg at the girth, which will encourage your horse to follow with its hindquarters.

A right-hand turn comes from the hand drawn to the right and increased pressure of the left leg.

Halting: a horse is said to be a "rear-engine vehicle," by which is meant that its power comes from its hindquarters. The lightning-like starts and turns a polo pony executes are all initiated by its hindquarters.

Rider position: two players in pursuit of the ball. The white-shirted player on the right is in better balance with his pony than his opponent, who is riding "behind the motion" of his pony's galloping stride. (Harold Roth/Equine Images)

Preparing your pony for these quick bursts of energy requires coordination of your hands and legs. Using just your hands will cause your pony to shift his weight forward; he will have to move his weight back onto his hocks before moving off again. Although your hands (through the reins to the bit) are the primary means of telling your pony to halt, your legs play an equally important role. Pressure against your pony's sides encourages him to bring his hindquarters under him in a square and balanced halt.

Flying changes of lead: polo ponies would waste valuable time changing leads at the gallop by slowing to a trot before striking off again on the correct lead. Instead, they have been taught to do flying changes, or to switch their sequence of footfalls in midair.

Although polo ponies have made this skill a reflex, you can encourage the transition by means of rein and leg pressure. Let's say you are cantering in a counterclockwise direction, your pony traveling on its left lead (the sequence of footfalls are as follows: right hind, left hind and right foreleg simultaneously, then left foreleg). To encourage your pony to swap to its right lead, increase the pressure on its right rein to start the turn to the right. At the same time, ask for a canter depart with your left leg behind the girth, and shift your seat slightly to the left to reinforce your leg.

The appropriate time to ask is when your pony's right hind leg has just left the ground, during the upward-and-forward phase of the cantering motion. That will give the pony enough time to react to your cues, landing with its left hind leg beginning the new sequence.

In the other direction (a flying change to the left lead), simply reverse the above aids—turn your pony's head to the left while asking for a canter depart with your right leg.

Leads: this pony is galloping on its left lead, as evidenced by its left foreleg in the air while its right foreleg and left hind leg are striking the ground simultaneously. (Harold Roth/Equine Images)

Four

The Basic Strokes

There is no better example of the phrase "operating in a vacuum" than trying to learn a sport from a book. Some sort of on-site practical experience is essential. Nevertheless, the "textbook approach" to learning a skill has its own advantages, not the least of which is being able to analyze concepts and procedures by breaking them down into their component parts.

Many people just starting out are fortunate enough to have access to a practice cage, an enclosed area that contains a wooden horse on which they can experience the sensation of being mounted. Others have gone directly to a live animal. Although there are those who learn the basic strokes while standing on the ground (and using a short mallet with a cut-down shaft), the following instructions will be directed at players who are sitting on a wooden, if not a flesh-and-blood, horse.

The left side of a horse is referred to as the near side, since most work around horses is traditionally done by a person standing on that side of a horse (for example, we tack and untack a horse and mount and dismount from the left). By the same token, the animal's right side is called the off side. Since players hold their mallets in their right hand, off-side strokes are the more natural and comfortable and, therefore, easier to learn. Therefore, let's begin with the off-side forehand and the backhand.

The Grip

Gripping the mallet involves first positioning its strap around your wrist. There are two ways, both beginning with the toe of the mallet head pointing toward you.

The first method is to pass your right hand through the strap, then twirl the mallet several times until the strap fits snugly around your wrist (but not so tight that it cuts off the circulation). The alternative, useful for shorter straps, is to put only your thumb through the loop, then pass the strap around the back of your hand. Do not, however, twist the strap around your thumb, since that can lead to a severely wrenched finger.

As for the grip itself, grasp the mallet handle as if you were shaking hands with the handle, with your index, middle, and ring fingers holding the mallet firmly but comfortably as the handle rests against your palm. Your thumb belongs on the top of the handle, directly across from the knuckles of the other fingers.

If you are using a pistol-grip handle, its bulge separates your index finger from your middle finger, as if your index finger were against a trigger.

The Rest Position

All strokes begin when the mallet is in the rest, or vertical position, just as the mallet should be held in this fashion when it is not being used for stroking. There are two reasons why. First, carrying the mallet at the vertical puts less of a strain on the player's right arm than if it were held at any angle other than approximately 90 degrees ("approximately" because the mallet will shift somewhat as it is carried along at speed). Equally important, this position avoids the danger of the mallet hitting other players and tripping up ponies.

With the reins in your left hand, grip the mallet comfortably with your right hand and raise the mallet head to an upright position. Your hand belongs just above your right knee, with your forearm parallel to the ground and your elbow in at (but not against) your side. Your wrist should be held naturally, with a slightly outward bend. If the mallet suddenly feels heavier, chances are that it is not perfectly vertical, so make sure the mallet shaft and head have not tilted forward, or to the rear, or to either side.

The Brace

As in tennis and golf, your body will play as important a role in stroking the ball as your arm does. To maximize the full use of your entire body, you must learn to hit from a standing position.

That position is called the **brace** (see photo, page 00), and as the name implies, it affords a solid foundation for your upper body. Still with the mallet in the rest position, rise in the stirrups until your seat clears the saddle. Force your weight into the stirrups, and maintain your balance by bracing your knees and thighs against your pony's sides. (Riders who have a hunter-seat equitation background will find the position somewhat similar to the half-seat, although your

The brace position in action: the player who is about to strike the ball has risen into the brace position for an off-side forehand shot, with his right stirrup bearing his weight. (Harold Roth/Equine Images)

upper-body position should be more at the vertical than when in the jumping position.)

Now twist your hips and rotate your upper body to the right until your shoulders are parallel to your pony's body and you are facing 90 degrees to the right. If you feel yourself slipping forward or backward, force more weight into your stirrups, keep your rib cage erect, and don't grip your knees so tight that you tend to hunch over. You may, if you wish, help keep your balance by placing your left hand on your pony's withers.

As you turn to face right, the majority of your weight should sink through your hips onto the right stirrup. Similarly, turning to the left will place more weight in that iron. If you feel your foot slipping in the stirrup, be sure that your feet are "well home," the arches of your feet against the stirrup treads.

The Off-Side Forehand

When you've mastered this hip/upper body flexibility, you'll be ready to learn the off-side forehand stroke.

The purpose of this stroke is to drive the ball in a forward direction (see photo, page 34). The motion is akin to a pitcher's underhand delivery in softball. Similar to that softball pitcher's delivery, the forehand is a sweeping motion, the way a second hand moves around the face of a clock. Just as a softball pitcher releases the ball when it is slightly ahead of his leg, so the polo player makes contact with the ball in a forehand when his mallet head is in front of his right leg (more specifically, at a point on line with his pony's right shoulder). And, even more than in a softball pitcher's release, the mallet head continues in a follow-through (here the analogy would be to a tennis forehand or a golf shot).

Unlike a pitcher, who keeps the ball close to his body during the delivery, the mallet must be kept away from the pony's side to avoid tripping up the animal—thus, the brace position.

The comparison to a clock's second hand is useful in trying to visualize the entire off-side forehand stroke. Think of the pony's head as 9:00, a point over the player's head as noon, the pony's tail as 3:00, and a point below the pony's girth as 6:00. The mallet head sweeps in a clockwise arc that begins at 11:00, then goes around the imaginary dial to make contact with the ball at approximately 7:00, finishing up with a follow-through that ends at 12:00.

Although the stroke is executed in one continuous motion, it is helpful to break it down into component parts.

1.   Start in the rest position. Tilt the mallet forward until its head is slightly ahead of your hand. Focus your eyes on an imaginary ball resting on the ground at a contact point approximately 2 feet to the right and slightly ahead of your right stirrup.

2.   Move into the brace position, rotating your upper body to the right. Simultaneously, raise your right hand up and back until your hand is slightly above your head. Your forearm should be approximately parallel to the ground, with your elbow pointed back

The contact point: the player is likely to stroke the ball at the optimum contact point for an off-side forehand, just when the ball is several feet in front of his pony's right shoulder. (Harold Roth/Equine Images)

toward your pony's tail. (If balancing is a problem, you may, if you wish, keep your rein hand braced on your pony's withers throughout the forehand stroke.)

3. Finish rotating your upper body to the point that your left shoulder points at the ball. Lean well off your pony and over the ball. Keep the majority of your weight in your right stirrup; your right toe pointed out, up to 90 degrees away from your pony's side, will help your leg support that weight. Bend your left leg back to help maintain your balance.

4. The mallet head builds up its velocity as you straighten your right arm; think of it as opening your elbow angle. It's a swinging motion, as if you were hitting a golf ball. Your right arm should be fully extended when it reaches a 2:00 position on the imaginary clock dial, with a straight line from upper arm to forearm to mallet shaft to mallet head (see photo, page 36).

5. The next phase of the swing, from 2:00 around the dial to 7:00, is to bring the mallet head to its maximum momentum. As your arm moves rearward and then downward, your head must keep stationary as a sort of pivot, with your eyes firmly fixed on the ball.

Your arm remains fully extended, with your wrist and elbow firmly, but not rigidly, locked to support the mallet. Think of the mallet as an extension of your arm, with your wrist on line with, not leading, the mallet head. Keep your wrist firm yet not tense, and let the balls of your index and middle fingers become the driving force of a smooth, continuous stroke.

Smooth means just that; stroking a ball does not mean pushing or punching or trying to "kill" it with as much force as you can muster. The trick is to build up the momentum by a smooth, fluid backswing, so that the momentum of the mallet head can do its work.

Equally important is to stay in the brace position, leaning well over your pony. Anything less will cause the mallet shaft or head to come in contact with your pony, at best deflecting the shot and at worst tripping up the animal.

6. By this point, your clock-hand arm-and-mallet combination has moved around the dial from its original 11:00 to approximately 6:00. As your arm approaches the 7:00 contact point, you will feel your wrist and forearm turn slightly outward. That's perfectly natural, and you should do nothing to resist this hitting-from-the-inside-out movement.

The mallet head should be several inches above the ground at the contact point. If it hits the ground before that point, you are leaning over too far. If (as is more likely) it sweeps too far above the ground, you have not leaned over far enough. In either case, make the appropriate adjustment in your brace position.

7. The follow-through (see photo, page 38) is an integral part of the stroke, as essential in polo as it is in golf or tennis, for the follow-through will determine how the ball will come off the mallet.

The off-side forehand: here, the player appears to have begun his stroke without having risen fully into the brace position. Nor is the player's weight over the pony's center of gravity. Accordingly, and in all likelihood, the shot will not travel with optimum velocity, distance, or accuracy. (Harold Roth/Equine Images)

The off-side forehand: another view of this fundamental stroke. The player's arm is fully extended, allowing the force of the mallet stroke to set the ball in motion. Note that the player's eyes are on the ball, and that he is not relying on rein contact to maintain his position in the saddle. (Harold Roth/Equine Images)

Keeping the clock analogy, the stroke continues past the 7:00 contact point until the mallet head points almost to noon. The follow-through should continue on the same plane as the downstroke. If you find the mallet brushing against your pony's neck, you may not have continued the inside-out movement.

Your eyes, which have remained focused on the ball until this point, should not start to look for the ball until you have finished your follow-through. As in golf, bringing your head up too soon will alter the stroke.

The off-side forehand: the dark-shirted player's stroke has reached the follow-through stage (the ball is visible to the left of the opposing player's head). (Harold Roth/Equine Images)

8. Once you finish the follow-through, return from the brace position to your seat in the saddle and return your mallet to the rest position.

Hitting the Off-Side Forehand

After you have practiced the stroke to your satisfaction, it's time to work on hitting a stationary ball.

With a ball at the contact point on the ground, start by taking half-shots, which means drawing your mallet back only 3 or 4 feet behind the ball. Meet the ball cleanly and smoothly, striking the lower half of the ball with the center of the mallet head below the shaft. (Hitting the upper half of the ball will result in a "topped" shot that "dinks" away.) Your grip should be firm enough so that the mallet does not alter its position in your hand. Your follow-through should take the mallet another 3 or 4 feet beyond the point of contact.

Moving up to taking full swings should not present any problems if you have mastered the earlier steps. Your goal remains to develop a smooth, consistent stroke by letting the momentum of the mallet head do its job.

The Off-Side Backhand

There are five components of the off-side backhand stroke.

1. The mallet position for the backhand is slightly different from how you have been holding your mallet for the forehand stroke. Holding your mallet in the rest position, turn your wrist a quarter-turn to the right until the first joints of your fingers are parallel to your pony's right side.

2. Raise your body into the brace position to the right. At the same time, carry your right hand across your chest until the mallet head drops over your left shoulder at an approximately 20-degree angle off the horizontal (in something of a back-scratching movement).

3. Point your right shoulder down toward the point of contact with the ball, which will be slightly behind your right heel. Your

upper body leans to the right. Your weight is in your right stirrup, with your left leg coming off your pony's side.

4. The downstroke phase begins by rotating your shoulders to the right while simultaneously straightening your right elbow and extending your arm as far as it can go. The sooner your arm reaches its full extension, the sooner the mallet head starts to gain momentum. Continue this downward arc in one smooth, continuous movement until you reach the contact point. Your thumb should provide the driving force.

5. Your upper body's rotation and the mallet head's momentum continue the stroke past the contact point into the follow-through, which ends when your right arm and shoulder are over your pony's right hip.

Hitting the Off-Side Backhand

As you've done with the off-side forehand, attempt to hit a ball back-hand only after you are comfortable with your stroke without a ball. Place the ball on the ground at the contact point, and start with several half-shots before going on to try full swings.

Five

Advanced Strokes

Watch a polo match in progress, and you will observe that not every stroke is taken on a player's off side. Players frequently approach the ball when it is on their ponies' near, or left side. There are also times when the ball should not be hit straight ahead or to the rear. These situations will require your adding other strokes to your repertoire—the near-side forehand and backhand, and the neck and the tail shot. Although you will have many opportunities to use them during play, they are considered advanced only in the sense that they should be learned after you have mastered the off-side forehand and backhand.

The Near-Side Forehand

1. Raise your mallet to the rest position. Give the grip a quarter-turn, as you do before hitting the off-side backhand, but here let the mallet head tilt at approximately 45 degrees to the left.

2. Rise into a brace position to the left, with your weight in your left stirrup and your shoulders parallel to the left side of your pony's body. Focus your eyes on the contact point where the ball would be, approximately 2 feet out from your pony's left shoulder.

3. Carry your right hand over your pony's body until your mallet is out beyond your head but at the same height as your left cheek. Maintain the bend in your right elbow as you lean out over your pony, and increase the rotation of your upper body until your right shoulder is pointing down toward the contact point.

4. Raise your right hand upward and as far back as you can, allowing your right shoulder to act as the pivot.

5. The downstroke begins as you let the mallet head's downward momentum straighten your elbow. Lean well over your pony's left side, with your shoulders remaining parallel to your pony's side. As in the off-side strokes, don't force the stroke, but let it happen naturally, with the ball of your thumb guiding the mallet from the thumb's position at the rear of the handle.

6. As the mallet head reaches the contact point, your right elbow should be straight and on line with your wrist and the mallet shaft.

7. Continue into a natural and smooth follow-through. Your arm will stop at approximately 45 degrees to the ground, but the mallet head's momentum will force a break in your wrist.

8. Return to the rest position.

The Near-Side Backhand

1.   Hold your mallet in the rest position, with your grip held as for the off-side forehand.

2.   As you rise into the brace position to the left, raise your right

The near-side forehand: the rider is in the brace position, his weight well in his left stirrup, and his right shoulder pointing toward the contact point with the ball. He has begun to straighten his right elbow, which allows the mallet head to follow down toward the ball. (Harold Roth/Equine Images)

The near-side forehand: another view shows the beginning of the stroke. The mallet head is well in advance of the player's head, and the player's shoulders are parallel to his pony's near side. (Harold Roth/Equine Images)

arm above your head, the mallet extended as far as it can, its head tilted back (your wrist will cock toward your shoulder). Sight in on the contact point approximately 2 feet out from and slightly ahead of your pony's left hind leg.

3. The downstroke begins as you rotate your shoulders, first by dropping your left shoulder, almost immediately followed by bringing your right shoulder around (here, your chest acts as the pivot point). Your right elbow remains straight.

4. Lean out over your pony so that your right arm clears your left hand and arm. Your weight is in your left stirrup, with your right leg off your pony's side.

5. The mallet head reaches the contact-point position, which is now slightly ahead of your left shoulder, and it continues back in a smooth follow-through. At the completion of the follow-through, your upper body will have rotated so far to the left that the most contact you feel against your pony comes from your right knee against the saddle flap.

6. Recover your balance and return to the rest position.

Up to now, you have been working on strokes that are intended to drive the ball straight ahead or straight behind you. Since there will be times when you will want the ball to travel obliquely, or in a diagonal direction, you will need to learn four additional strokes, the so-called neck and tail strokes.

The Off-Side Neck Stroke

This stroke will send the ball traveling obliquely to the left (if you think of your pony's body as pointing north on a compass, the ball will travel in a northwesterly direction).

1. Begin the stroke by assuming the brace position, but lean farther away off your pony's side than for an off-side forehand. Since the contact point with the ball will be closer to your pony's right shoulder than for a forehand, it is vital to lean far enough so that you can hit the ball in more of a right-to-left direction.

2. Simultaneously, extend your right arm until it is at a right angle to your pony's side. Your wrist should be cocked so that the mallet head points upward at a 45 degree angle to the ground.

The off-side neck stroke: note that the mallet head will make contact with the ball slightly ahead of the pony's right foreleg. (Harold Roth/Equine Images)

The off-side neck shot: this photo shows the follow-through. The player's wrist has reached below his pony's neck, and the player is ready to bring the mallet back. (Harold Roth/Equine Images)

3. Swing at the ball to hit it in the desired northwesterly direction. The mallet will pass under your pony's neck, your arm ending up against his neck. The force of your stroke and the "whippiness" of the shaft will force the mallet head to continue well under the pony's neck (See photo on page 47). Once the mallet head has gone as far as it is going to, swing the mallet back under your pony's neck and recover your balance in the saddle.

The Near-Side Neck Stroke

This stroke, which will send the ball obliquely to the right, begins with the rest and brace positions that you learned for the near-side forehand.

1. Lean well over your pony's left side as you draw the mallet head back, pointing your right shoulder down toward where the contact point will be (ahead and slightly off to the side of your pony's left shoulder).

2. Think to "swing out, then hit" in order to hit the ball in a northeasterly direction. Once the mallet head has made contact, the follow-through will make the shaft pass under your pony's neck. Your arm will make contact with the pony's neck or shoulder.

3. Once your follow-through is completed, bring the mallet back to the rest position and recover your position in the saddle.

Tail Strokes

The off-side and near-side tail strokes are mirror images of their respective neck strokes, sending the ball off in diagonal directions to the rear of your pony. Both are especially useful for clearing the ball in close quarters with opposing players.

The off-side tail stroke is made in much the same way as the off-side backhand, except that your left shoulder must come farther out over your pony's right side so you can face farther to the rear.

Similarly, the near-side tail stroke is something of an exaggerated near-side backhand, but with your left shoulder even farther out over your pony's left side. In both this and the off-side tail stroke, the contact point will be behind and a foot or so away from your pony's hind leg.

Push Stroke

The object of this off-side forehand is to move the ball only 10 or so yards to the left (for example, when you want to pass the ball to a teammate who is that far ahead and to that side of you). Instead of taking a full stroke, or even a half-stroke, simply push the mallet head against the ball, the impetus coming only from your elbow.

Blocking: out of position to stop the ball with an off-side stroke, the player is attempting a simple blocking maneuver by reaching down to stop the ball with his mallet head. (Harold Roth/Equine Images)

Between-The-Legs Stroke

To send the ball off in a perpendicular direction to the way your pony is facing, you will have to drive the ball under your pony's belly. As you can imagine, there is a very real danger of hitting one of his legs to the point of tripping him. Therefore, consider this stroke as kind of a "chip" shot with no follow-through. Although expert players are able to stop the mallet shaft with one of their own legs, beginning players are far better off making the mallet head hit the ground at the moment it reaches the contact point.

Six

Solo Drills

The next step, after you have gotten down the correct form for the basic and advanced strokes, is to move on to hitting a ball when first you, and then you and the ball, are in motion. (If you have been working in a practice cage, where the sloping floor lets a ball roll back to you, you might want to begin with the ball-in-motion material of this chapter.)

Working out on a pony is called "stick and ball." Players enjoy the drill for a variety of reasons, not the least of which is the chance to improve and maintain their coordination and sense of timing. At this stage of your training, the factor of player-and-pony-in-motion introduces one of those essential elements in what constitutes the perfect stroke, that of timing.

Timing means fundamentally coordinating your stroke so that your mallet head makes contact with the ball precisely when you want it to. There is, alas, no precise formula for when you should begin your stroke, so you will have to let practice help you develop your eye-hand coordination.

Begin with an off-side forehand. Walk your pony slowly up to where a ball rests on the ground. Two or three strides away from the ball, assume the brace position and bring your mallet back 3 or 4 feet to prepare for a half-stroke. Keeping your eyes on the ball, time the forward phase of the stroke so the mallet head meets the ball at the contact point along your pony's right shoulder. The operative word here is *meet*, since all you want to do is let your mallet head make solid contact.

Many beginners find that they hit late, or miss the ball completely (known informally as an air shot), when they aim at it. If over-riding the ball becomes a problem for you, aim for a contact point 1 or 2 feet in front of your right shoulder, and see whether that doesn't improve your timing.

The faster your pony moves, the sooner the contact point will come up, as you will discover when your pony approaches the ball at even just a faster walk. Accordingly, you will have to start your stroke that much sooner.

"Topping" is the term for hitting the upper half of the ball. The ball will move only a few feet, often bouncing off the mallet. You can hear, as well as feel and see, a topped shot—its sound is less than a solid "thwack." If that happens, you will need to lean farther over the ball to lower the contact point of your mallet head.

When you ride up to take a full off-side forehand, begin the down-swing when the ball is about 2 feet in front of your left shoulder. Precisely how long to keep the mallet head poised at its highest point before you begin the downstroke will depend on your pony's pace toward the ball. Some adjustments may be necessary before you get an eye for correct timing.

Hitting an off-side forehand from a canter will be the next step. A nice, easy lope is the pace to start with. If you find yourself meeting the ball when your pony's hind legs are hitting the ground (the feeling will be of being poised to spring forward), so much the better, for the animal's forward momentum helps to maximize driving the ball. However, you needn't be concerned about sequences of footfalls at this point—just work on meeting the ball.

A steady pace becomes especially important at the gallop. Keep your pony at the same speed as you move up to, meet, and pass beyond the contact point. Avoid the common tendency to slow down as you reach the ball. If you find this happening, you may be unconsciously anticipating the shot and conveying the anticipation to your pony by tensing the reins or relaxing your legs.

A word here about controlling your pony. Maintain a steady and even tension on the reins so you will be able to steer, since you won't have much chance of reaching the ball if your pony meanders away from or over the contact point. However, reins that are held too short create worse problems. A strangle hold interferes with your pony's pace, and you'll find that your pony will resist you at every stride. Just as bad is catching your pony in the mouth with a sharp jab on the reins, which is also another way to ruin the animal's enthusiasm for the game. If you have difficulty keeping your balance while stroking the ball, keep your left hand on your pony's withers for support.

Reins that are too long should be corrected too, as should any tendency to "drop" your pony with sudden breaks in rein contact, especially when you are about to stroke the ball.

Your pony may misinterpret any inadvertant movement of your left hand as a neck-reining cue, so be sure to keep it steady as you move up to the ball and make your strokes.

Your legs will also keep your pony on course toward the ball. A horse finds it most comfortable when its rider stays over its center of balance; they will instinctively move in the direction that riders lean, as if to move under their riders. Accordingly, as you lean over the right side to take off-side shots, you may feel your pony shift its weight. To compensate for that drift, keep your right lower leg against your pony's side to keep its hind end on a straight line. (That's nothing new, since you're already using that position for your own upper body support.)

After you have mastered the off-side forehand and backhand, turn your attention to these two strokes on the near side. (Many trainers have their students get into the habit of moving their ponies off to the left after the near-side backhand. The reason is one of safety, since there is all likelihood that another player will be riding up behind during a game.)

Hitting a Moving Ball

At some stage, just stroking a ball and watching it move away will lose its appeal. You'll be eager to gallop in pursuit—after all, isn't that what polo is all about?

(When this time comes will depend in large measure on your instructor's teaching methods. Some coaches prefer to wait until some or all the strokes have been learned using a stationary ball before having their students hit a moving one.)

The speed and direction of a moving ball add another set of variables to the equation. To keep things simple at the beginning, approach the ball at the walk and drive it forward with an off-side forehand. As soon as you have stroked the ball, urge your pony into a canter. Regulate the pony's speed so that you reach the ball while it is still moving, then begin the steps of taking another off-side forehand. Adjust the timing of your downstroke so that you will hit the ball at the correct contact point.

Several results may occur. You may send the ball traveling farther along in the same direction (on the same line, as polo players use the term). If so, you are justified in congratulating yourself on your timing. On the other hand, your stroke may land ahead of or behind the contact point. If that's the case, try again, starting with the preliminary first shot and making whatever adjustment you need to improve your timing. With practice, you'll be meeting the moving ball as cleanly and accurately as you were with the ball at rest.

Until now, we have not been overly concerned with direction.

As your stroke-making skills improve, however, you should begin to work on hitting the ball where you want it to go. Select a focus point in the distance, perhaps a goalpost or a tree or a point along an arena sideboard. See how close you can come to hitting the ball on a line toward that spot.

With regard to distance, it bears repeating that trying to hit the ball a country mile is not part of the fundamentals that you are developing. Just be assured that as you master the basics of stroking and develop your hand-eye coordination, you'll be pleased by the increase in distance and accuracy that you are able to achieve.

Drills

The most productive way to make use of your stick and ball practice time is to work in an organized, logical way. This will involve sets of exercises (as opposed to just hitting the ball all over the place). The following are widely used and effective drills.

—Alternate your strokes: alternate between near-side and off-side forehands up and back the length of the field or arena. Reverse your direction with backhands when you reach the ends.

—Follow two or three off-side forehands with an off-side backhand. Then turn and go back the other way with two or three near-side forehands, ending this time with a near-side backhand. Turn again and repeat from the beginning.

—Circle the ball in a clockwise direction around the field or arena, using only off-side forehands, then near-side forehands. Reverse to a counter-clockwise direction, first using off-side forehands before working on your near-side forehand.

—A basic solo practice drill, especially for indoor polo, is trying to score with off-side corner forehands. Work the ball to the right corner of the arena as you face an opponent's goal, then stroke a forehand between the posts or markers. The fact that your pony's body blocks the defenders gives you a decided advantage in an actual game, as does the chance to make an off-side forehand (the easiest and most reliable stroke). Working on making the most of these advantages will be rewarded during actual play.

Finally, a word or two about observation. Your coach will not only teach you correct form and position, but he or she will be looking for any errors of form and position that can crop up at any stage of a player's development. In addition to your responsibility to profit from your mentor's sharing his or her expertise, you should also assume the responsibility of what might be called independent research. That means no more (and no less) than watching other players practice, and having others watch you. Whether you are learning the game through private lessons, or a club or school program, take advantage of opportunities to observe the techniques of others. What are the good ones doing that make their stick work and horsemanship so good? By the same token, what errors can you spot? And in both instances, how can you relate what you're seeing to improve your own skills?

Seven

....

Practicing with Others

....

Polo is first and foremost a team sport, and you'll be eager to play with and against other people. But before you saddle up for your first game, you will need to know more than just how to execute a variety of strokes. That's why stick and ball practice with others is a valuable, and ongoing, part of any player's time spent in the saddle.

Drills with One Other Player

Stick and ball practice with others is almost always more enjoyable and often more profitable than working by yourself. Moreover, considering another person with whom you are practicing as a teammate is the first step in developing the essential sense of teamwork that a polo game demands.

Teamwork centers around passing the ball, as well as backing up a teammate, so you and another player will want to start out with these basic two-person drills.

—Spacing yourselves approximately 30 to 40 yards apart, you hit a forehand up to your partner and then turn 180 degrees. Your partner backhands the ball to you, and you return it with a backhand. In the meantime, your partner has turned so that he can respond with a forehand.

—Both of you start at one end of the playing area, with your partner starting off by driving the ball forward with a near-side forehand. You ride ahead to take the second shot. Your teammate follows so that if you miss, he is there to back you up (keep going if you miss, so you will be downfield to receive his backup shot). If you make contact, your teammate gallops on by for his turn.

Continue this alternating-shot drill down the field, taking care not to cross each other's lines.

The point where a next shot will carry the ball over the end line (or against the end wall) is the time to reverse. If it is your shot, call out "turn!" before taking a backhand, while your teammate checks to see whether you make contact with the ball. If so, you both turn downfield and continue the drill going the other way. If not, you make your turn and head downfield to receive your teammate's backup backhand.

—As your partner gallops upfield, hit a forehand that will lead him when he has reached a spot some 30 yards ahead of you. Do not follow, but halt and wait for your partner to back the ball to you, at which time you ride up to meet it and once again drive the ball ahead of your partner, who will again back the ball to you.

—Starting out approximately 20 yards ahead of your partner, you hit two short forehands, then intentionally miss the third. As you continue downfield, your partner backs you up with two short forehands of his own before intentionally missing the third attempt. By that time you have turned 180 degrees so you can ride toward the ball. Hit two forehands and then intentionally missing a third, repeat the drill in the other direction.

—A variation of the foregoing is to ride off to the right or left after you have missed your third shot, so your partner will have the practice of finding a moving target for his backhanders.

—You and your partner space yourselves 20 yards apart at the right end of the playing area. Work the ball upfield by passing it with strokes angled at 45 degrees. The player on the right will be hitting off-side forehands, while the other one will be using near-side forehands. Work on leading each other so that your ponies will not need sudden bursts of speed or checking.

When you and your partner have reached the far end of the playing area, reverse your direction with a backhand, then work the ball downfield. Switch sides of the field, so that the player who has been hitting off-side forehands now has the chance to hit them off his pony's near side.

All the foregoing drills should be repeated with you and your partner alternating positions, for equal opportunities for working at the other player's position.

Beginning players tend to favor their off-side strokes, since hitting the ball from the right side seems more natural (and therefore safer) than from the left side. If you think this way, nip this bad habit in the bud now. Work on your near-side strokes during these drills until you become comfortable and confident.

This is also the time to continue to work on accurate strokes. Accuracy here means hitting the ball where you intend it to go. If your shots consistently veer off to the left or right, check your grip, brace, and/or downstroke form. Your coach will have valuable suggestions, and if the problem persists, don't hesitate to go back to square-one basics and correct the cause.

Drills With More Than Two Others

Group practice involving more than just you and another player will introduce more advanced modes of play. Four players doing two-on-two drills will necessarily become involved in both offensive and defensive techniques.

RIDING OFF

You and an opposing player on your right are both in pursuit of the ball. He has the line, and you see that you cannot get to the ball without crossing that line. What can you do? Ride him off the ball.

Riding off is the term for pushing an opponent out of the way (actually, it's your pony that will do the pushing). It is accomplished by positioning your pony against your opponent's mount so that your pony can use its impulsion and momentum. Contact can be either a single bump or a succession of them, depending on how long you want to — and are able to — immobilize your opponent (See photo on page 61).

The maxim "First the man, then the line, and then the ball" determines your order of priorities. You must first judge your opponent's speed and direction so that your leg makes impact just in front of his. Approaching too fast may cause the impact to be made against the other horse's shoulder or even farther forward, which is a foul. Similarly, coming in too slowly may force your knee to touch behind your opponent's saddle, which is also a foul.

Your position in the saddle during this approach should be over your pony's center, using your hands to direct and your outside leg to urge your pony toward its target.

Since riding off requires a pony to be balanced, it is important that your mount is on the correct lead. If contact is to be made from the right (that is, on your opponent's near side), your pony needs to be on its right lead at the moment of contact. Conversely, your pony should be on its left lead in order to drive your opponent to the left.

Your pony need not do all the work. Once contact has been made, and if you have the opportunity, you can hinder your opponent by leaning your shoulder against his upper body. You may use only your shoulder, since using your elbow or mallet is a foul.

Remember "First the man, then the line, and then the ball." Only after you have made contact and ridden your opponent off the line should you turn your attention to the ball, if it is within stroking distance.

There will be other instances where your objective is not to take a shot. You may wish only to prevent your opponent from hitting so that one of your teammates can come up behind for a better shot than you can make. In such cases, a single bump at a sharper angle than that for coming up alongside and maintaining prolonged contact will be appropriate.

Riding off does not give unrestricted license to inflict damage on other players, and the relevant rules protect against dangerous impact. When riding another player off at speed (meaning at the gallop), you may approach from only a 45-degree angle or less, since a greater angle would increase the likelihood of a broadside collision and a pony falling.

Riding off: the dark-shirted Number Two player is riding off his opponent. His pony's shoulder has made contact with the opposing pony's shoulder in front of the saddle, and the player's right leg is driving his pony's body over to force the opposing player away from the line of play. (Harold Roth/Equine Images)

There is an exception to this rule. Moving at slow speeds, such as during a throw-in or at other times when ponies are at the walk, you may bump another player at up to a 90-degree angle, as there is little danger that the force of impact would cause his pony to fall.

You may not, however, ride an opponent off dangerously across the line of the ball; nor can two players "gang up" and ride off an opponent (two-on-one is a foul at any time).

The best way to become accustomed to physical contact with another player is to begin at the walk. Move slowly up to and against a stationary (and cooperative) pony and rider. Work on getting your knee in front of your opponent's, and lean into his upper body. Only when you feel secure doing this at the walk should you try it at the canter, then gallop, against a moving opponent.

Rules of the Road

Even the most casual, noncompetitive play has the potential to create potentially hazardous situations. Polo has very definite "rules of the road" that promote the safety of players and ponies. They are observed in even the most casual encounters with two or more players. It is never too early in any player's career to learn these rules, and to get into the habit of observing them.

Crossing the line: you hit an off-side forehand, then gallop after it to take a follow-up shot. Another player comes alongside and tries to pass you while someone else gallops across the field or arena to head off the ball. Who has the right-of-way?

You do, but only as long as you hit the ball in the line in which you are traveling. When you hit your first shot, you establish the line of the ball. As long as you remain on that line, you have possession of the ball. Any other player who cuts in front of you close enough to constitute a potentially dangerous situation has crossed your line and thus committed a foul (See drawing on page 63).

What constitutes crossing the line close enough to create a danger is a matter of judgment; the rule is not written in terms of precise distance, since distance will depend on the pace that the ponies are traveling, as well as the angle of possible impact. The best rule of thumb, in lieu of practical demonstrations by your coach, is that if a situation appears to present a hazard, don't cross the line.

It is possible, however, to lose your right to the line even though you are the last player to hit the ball. If you veer away, even if you return to the line, you lose the line relative to another player who has been riding behind you and has stayed on the line.

Riding to meet: you hit an off-side forehand and gallop down the field or arena after the ball. You glance up and see another player galloping directly toward the ball in front of you. Who must give way?

Both of you. In order to avoid a collision, two players who are riding at a ball in the open must both give way to the left. Either of you may try to hit the ball, but only with an off-side forehand.

In arena play, however, if the ball is traveling alongside a wall, you as the last player to hit the ball have the right-of-way, and you may try to hit the ball with either an off- or near-side stroke.

Crossing the imaginary line of the ball in front of an opponent. (Sam Savitt illustration)

Riding on the line: the player in white is riding on the line that the ball is traveling. He has the right-of-way, and to avoid crossing that imaginary line—and thus committing a foul—the defending player has started to neck-rein his pony off to the right. (Harold Roth/Equine Images)

HOOKING

Your opponent, who is on your right, begins a near-side forehand, but you are not in position to ride him off without committing a foul. What can you do?

You can hook, or reach out with your mallet and try to snag or otherwise deflect the other player's mallet head. Hooking may be done on both the near and off side, as long as you are on the same side of your opponent as the ball is. It is an important part of every player's defensive game, and you should learn to become adept at this stick work.

First of all, you must be near enough to your opponent to be able to intercept his mallet during its downswing phase of the stroke (high

Hooking: a well-executed example of this defensive maneuver. The Number Four player has made contact with his opponent's mallet below the pony's rump (any higher point of contact will result in a foul). (Harold Roth/Equine Images)

hooking, when an opponent's mallet head is above his shoulder, is a foul).

How to hook depends on the circumstances and personal preference. Some players simply point their mallet in the general direction of the path that they anticipate their opponent's stroke will take. Others give their mallet a light swing, as if to hit the ball themselves. Slashing, however, is dangerous and is penalized accordingly.

When and where to make contact depends on your position in relation to your opponent. If at all possible, make contact when his mallet head is below his pony's knee; your opponent will have already committed himself to making his stroke. If, however, you are unable to reach that zone, make your hook whenever his mallet head is below his pony's rump (hooking any higher is illegal, since the mallet head will be above your opponent's shoulder). (See photo on page 65.)

Hooking an opponent's off-side strokes when you are on his right is more difficult than going for his near-side ones, since your pony is between you and your opponent. The most appropriate maneuver would be to ride him off, since you may not reach your mallet under a pony (yours or an opponent's) or across your opponent's pony. Both maneuvers are dangerous and constitute rule violations.

As with riding off, practice hooking first at the walk, and then at faster speeds.

Other Rule Violations

As you begin playing with others, you will need to learn about additional prohibitions against dangerous conduct. The following apply regardless of whether done against an opponent or a teammate.

—Striking another player or pony with your mallet.
—Stroking a ball at close quarters so that it hits another pony's legs.
—Positioning your pony in order to use the animal to block a shot or ball.
—Swerving from side to side in front of another player (zig-zagging).
—Pulling up in front of or across from another player on the right-of-way.
—Running into or over another pony's rear quarters.

Even though practice work seldom includes a referee who will call violations—or perhaps *because* there is no referee—it is the responsibility of all players to observe the rules of polo. Violations during a match result in penalties (which will be discussed in Chapter Eight), but at this stage of your polo career, learning which maneuvers are permissible and which are not is as important a part of your education as learning and perfecting the strokes.

Advanced Drills

The most basic two-on-two drill starts when you and your teammate, as the offense, position yourselves at one end of the field or arena. As you work the ball downfield, the other team tries to take over possession. Here, accurate passing becomes crucial on the offense, as do riding off and hooking whenever the other team gets the ball.

This is a good time to get into the habit of communicating with your teammate (or teammates, when you have more than one partner). Let your teammates know where the ball is going if you are in a position to see or otherwise know. Shout "center" or "boards" whenever appropriate, and "turn!" when the flow of play heads in the other direction. When you have the chance to make a backhand, yell "turn!" before you take the stroke if you are confident of making it.

You may find yourself in a situation where three more experienced players are looking for a fourth to join them in a scrimmage, but you don't feel all that confident about your mallet work. A very valuable way to experience the flow of play and to practice defensive maneuvers is to join in, but without carrying a mallet. This is a way to concentrate on learning to mark, or stay with, an opposing player and to ride him off, all without having to be concerned about moving the ball. Most veteran players, who are eager to encourage novices' education, will be happy to oblige.

Eight

Team Play

In the course of stick and ball practice with other players, you will discover that you have developed particular skills and enthusiasms. Perhaps you are adept at hitting the "long ball." You may especially enjoy the close contact of riding off an opponent, or perhaps you find that opportunities to score are less important than the satisfaction of preventing the opposition from scoring. Although all facets of the game are important, certain abilities and preferences can in large measure determine the position to which you will be assigned when you play a game. (More realistically, however, a novice who joins more experienced players is normally assigned to play as either the Number One or as the Back, since the Two and Three positions require greater skill and experience.)

The polo analogy to "hockey on horseback" goes beyond the fact that both sports involve moving a ball or puck with a stick. Watch a hockey game, and you will see that the players have responsibilities when on offense and defense (some readers may be old enough to remember that before football's two-platoon and, more recently, its special-teams systems were instituted, everyone played both ways in that sport too).

Polo makes similar demands, and the position you play will determine your primary duties when your team has possession of the ball, as well as when the other team does.

The four positions of an outdoor polo team are called the Number One, Number Two, Number Three, and Number Four, or Back. These designations refer to the players' relative positions during play. Number One ranges closest to the other team's goal, ahead of Number Two (in that sense, they are both considered their team's "forwards"). Number Three ranges ahead of the Back, who stays closest to his own team's goal (the Number Three and the Back are considered "backs" in relation to the "forwards").

Number One: this player spearheads his team's attack. On offense, a One has two basic options—to slip past the defending Back and wait for a pass and the chance to score, or to block the Back by riding the defender off away from the goal (and by so doing permit his Number Two teammate to score).

The One remains upfield on defense, riding off the opposing Back while preparing to resume the attack as soon as his team regains possession of the ball.

Number Two: as an offensive attack develops, the Two receives passes from his teammates behind him. Once he has received the ball, he has his own options—to pass the ball up to his One, or to keep the ball himself (the latter makes sense if One is marked, or covered, by the defending Back).

On defense, the Two covers the other team's Number Three player, looking for chances to forestall offensive attacks.

Number Three: players holding this position are the pivots of their teams. A Three initiates all attacks by driving the ball up to his team's "forward" players (perhaps even more than with Twos, a strong aggressive attitude is a prerequisite).

A Three's responsibilities on defense also require boldness and versatility. They include covering the opponents' Two, seizing opportunities to turn the play, and assisting his Back in defending against a score.

Teamwork and team play: while the Number One dark-shirted player follows the ball, his Number Two and Number Three teammates pick up their men. (Harold Roth/Equine Images)

The Back: like a goalie in hockey, the Back's primary responsibility is to prevent the other team from scoring. In that regard, being able to hit consistently long backhands is essential.

Equally important is being able to mark the opposing Number One, preventing him from slipping by to receive passes and score.

With regard to arena, or indoor, polo, where teams consist of three players, the positions are the Number One, Number Two (who combines the roles of outdoor polo's Numbers Two and Three), and the Back.

The foregoing duties and responsibilities, it should be stressed, outline the players' *primary* roles. There will be times during a game that players interchange their positions, such as when a teammate has been ridden off or is otherwise out of position. When this happens, this rearrangement should be maintained until there is a logical time for the players so involved to go back to their original positions.

Goal! A player following his shot through the goalposts. (Harold Roth/Equine Images)

Team Tactics

THE THROW-IN

The throw-in is the situation that players most often face. It occurs at the beginning of each chukker, as well as when play resumes after a goal, or when the ball goes out of bounds over the sideboards.

At the start of a throw-in, both teams line up in a row side by side, waiting for the referee to bowl the ball between the two rows. All players must remain stationary, with their mallets held down on their off sides. Although it is not always done, the Number One players of both teams line up next to each other closest to the referee, with the Number Twos, the Number Threes, and the Backs behind them in that order.

As a Number One, you will be the first to have the chance to

The throw-in begins each chukker. (Sam Savitt illustration)

get the ball. Watch the referee's arm to see when the ball is released, then time your mallet work to gain possession. If you do get the ball, send it toward your opponent's goal. If the opposing Number One gets the ball, stay with him, either hooking his mallet or riding him off to spoil his opportunity for a shot.

There will be times when the ball passes beyond you, at which point you should immediately move toward your opponent's goal and mark the opposing Back.

If you are playing at the Number Two position, your job is to stop the ball in the event that it passes by the Number Ones. If it continues beyond you, turn and mark the opposing Number Three.

As a Number Three (or Back, in arena play), take control of the ball if it reaches you. Otherwise, follow the ball with the intention of getting control, hitting a backhand if the other team has possession.

Sometimes the ball will roll all the way through to the Number Four. In such instances, the Number Four should pass the ball out to a teammate, then remain downfield (relative to the other players) to defend against an offensive drive by the opposing team.

THE HIT-IN

A hit-in is the method by which, in outdoor polo, a team brings the ball back into play after the other team has hit it out of bounds over the end line. The referee places the ball on the end line, and the Back is the player who customarily rides up to take the stroke.

Some teams develop set plays that they use on hit-ins, such as fanning out then coming back into a line as the ball is returned to play (the idea is to surprise the opposing team). These strategies maintain players' assigned relative positions (as Numbers One, Two, Three, and Back), as well as assure that there is someone to back up the hitter.

Whether or not your team uses such plays, the general advice to keep moving applies here. Instead of waiting until the ball reaches or passes you before you put your pony into motion, start moving as soon as the Back moves up toward the ball.

Defending against the other team's hit-in will place you in a field position where an interception can easily lead to a score. With this in mind, the defending team's players should be on a constant lookout for such an opportunity.

GENERAL TACTICS ON OFFENSE

Always be aware of where you and all the other players are in relation to the ball and to the goals. Learn to anticipate where they are going and what they are planning to do. Good chess players think several moves ahead, and you should develop a similar skill.

If you don't have a chance to get at the ball, ride off or bump the opponent whom you are responsible for marking. That will make one fewer defender for your teammate who has the ball to contend with. That means staying up with your opponent. Don't let him get ahead of you or slip behind.

Communicate with your teammates. If you think you have a better shot at the ball than a teammate ahead of you, shout "leave it!" (similarly, hearing "leave it!" from a teammate is a signal to do just

Melee: after a throw-in where no one gained outright possession, both teams converge on the loose ball. (Harold Roth/Equine Images)

that—instead, take out your opponent). By the same token, stay far enough away from your teammates so you will be ready to receive passes.

Keep moving. It's easier to keep an eye on the ball and the flow of play when you are in motion.

GENERAL TACTICS ON DEFENSE

The primary responsibility of all players on defense is to stop your opposing player from hitting the ball, not just from scoring. Ride him off, or, when appropriate, hook his mallet to prevent him from delivering or receiving a pass.

If you have the chance to "back the ball," (that is, reverse the ball's direction) back it away toward the open portion of the field or arena, never toward oncoming ponies.

Whether to pick up a nearby opponent who has managed to slip away from one of your teammates depends on a variety of factors, not the least of which is that abandoning the player you are assigned to cover will give him a chance to get the ball. If a teammate shouts for you to switch, stay with the new opponent until you are able to return to your regular assignment without jeopardizing your team's defense.

Penalties

As discussed in the preceding chapter, rule violations such as crossing the line of the ball, illegal hooking, and dangerous riding will be penalized. Penalties, which depend on the infraction and/or its severity, can range from automatic goals to free hits from various distances against a defended or an undefended goal. In that respect, you should become familiar with the relevant sections of the Rules of Play.

The player who has been fouled is not necessarily the one who will take the penalty shot; that job belongs to the team's most capable hitter. If he scores, play resumes with a throw-in; otherwise, play immediately continues.

The role of the hitter's teammates is twofold—to be prepared to follow the shot in the event that a goal is not scored, as well as to be prepared to defend against the other team's gaining possession of the ball.

In those instances when a team may defend against a penalty shot, all defending players must position themselves a specific distance away from the ball. For a 60-yard penalty, they must be behind the 30-yard line; for 30- and 40-yard penalties, they must be behind the back line (but not between the goalposts). Once positioned, they may not move until the ball has been hit. Then the best (that is, the most reliable) technique is to first block the ball with the mallet, instead of immediately trying to hit the ball away with a full stroke.

Crossing the line of the ball in these situations should be avoided, not only to prevent a penalty being called, but to reduce the likelihood of dangerous collisions.

Skill at team play comes from more than merely being able to hit the ball. Developing a "polo sense" is the result of many hours of playing, of having experienced as many possible situations as this multi-faceted sport offers. Be prepared to make mistakes, but regard any errors of judgment or missed opportunities to have anticipated the flow of play as learning experiences, then profit from them.

The importance of communication cannot be stressed too much. Being a team player includes a willingness to obey the instructions of your teammates, especially the team captain. Make sure you know exactly what vocal commands your team uses, from the most common "turn!" and "mark your man!," to more complicated commands that indicate specific strategies and plays. And if you're not sure or you don't remember, don't be embarrassed to ask.

Observation will always be an ongoing element in your education. As you watch others play—and it doesn't matter whether it's a low-goal game or a high-goal match—watch more than just the ball. Try to catch the rhythm and flow of the game. Let yourself be analytical. Look for patterns of positioning, and see how the better players are able to immobilize their opponents, then capitalize on scoring opportunities. Equally important is watching a game with a critical eye—learning to spot and understand the reasons for missed opportunities will be extremely useful in developing your own sense of team play.

(Ross A. Benson)

Nine

....

Where To Find Polo

....

Whether at the club, intercollegiate, or tournament level, there are literally hundreds of places in the United States and abroad where you can enjoy polo as a spectator or participant.

Polo Clubs in the United States and Canada

UNITED STATES

ALABAMA
Blue Water Creek Polo Club, Muscle Shoals
Mobile Point Clear Polo Club, Mobile

(*Ross A. Benson*)

ARIZONA

Camelback Polo Club, Scottsdale
Krazy Horse Polo Club, Scottsdale
La Mariposa Polo Club, Tucson
Paradise Valley Polo Club, Cave Creek
Pima County Polo Club, Tucson

CALIFORNIA

Central Valley Polo Club, Turlock
Eldorado Polo Club, Palm Desert
Fair Hill Polo and Hunt Club, Topanga
Garrod Polo Farms, Saratoga
Greenbriar Polo Club, Sacramento
K and T Ranch Polo Club, Grass Valley
LaJolla Polo Club, LaJolla
Los Angeles Polo Club, Los Angeles
Malibu Polo Club, Malibu
Mad River Polo Club, Korbel
Menlo Polo Club, Menlo Park
Modesto Polo Club, Modesto
Moorpark Polo Club, Moorpark
Napa Polo Club, San Francisco
Pebble Beach Polo Club, Pebble Beach
Rancho Delux, Arroyo Grande
Sacramento Valley Polo Club, Sacramento
Sagebrush Polo Club, Litchfield
San Mateo-Burlingame Polo Club, San Mateo
Santa Barbara Polo Club, Santa Barbara
Santa Rosa Polo Club, Santa Rosa
Tri Valley Polo Club, Encino
Will Rogers Polo Club, Los Angeles
Winston Polo Club, Anaheim

COLORADO

Aspen Polo Club, Aspen
Cattle Creek Polo Club, Aspen
Plum Creek Polo Club, Sedalia
Red Rock Rangers Polo Club, Monument

CONNECTICUT

Fairfield County Hunt Club, Westport
Greenwich Polo Club, Greenwich
Ox Ridge Hunt Club, Darien

Salem Valley Polo Club, Salem
Shallowbrook Polo Club, Somers

DISTRICT OF COLUMBIA

National Capital Park Polo Club, Washington, DC

FLORIDA

Central Florida Polo Club, Carcona
Fairlane Farms, West Palm Beach
Gulfstream Polo Club, Lake Worth
Ocala Polo Club, Ocala
Orlando Polo Club, Orlando
Palm Beach Polo and Country Club, West Palm Beach
Polo Club of Jacksonville, Jacksonville
Royal Palm Polo Club, Boca Raton
Tampa Bay Polo Club, Temple Terrace
U-Bet Land & Cattle Co. Polo Club, Brandon

GEORGIA

Atlanta Polo Club, Atlanta
Columbus Polo Club, Columbus
Foxhall Polo Club, Carrollton
Golden Isles Polo Club, St. Simeon Isle

HAWAII

Hawaii Polo Club at Mokuleia, Honolulu
Kauai Polo Club, Lihue Kauai
Manua Kea Polo Club, Kamuela
Maui Polo Club, Kahului
Tongg Ranch Polo Club, Honolulu

IDAHO

Sun Valley Polo Club, Sun Valley

ILLINOIS

Glendale Polo Club, Glen Ellyn
Green Valley Polo Club, Naperville
Healy Farms Polo Club, Northbrook
Midwest Polo Center, Naperville
Naperville Women's Polo Club, Naperville
Oak Brook Polo Club, Oak Brook
Peoria Polo Club, Chillicothe
Rockford Polo Club, Rockford

INDIANA
Longwood Polo Club, Carmel

IOWA
Des Moines Polo Club, Des Moines
Iowa City Polo Club, Iowa City

KANSAS
Fairfield Polo Assn., Wichita

KENTUCKY
Hardscuffle Polo Club, Louisville
Kentucky Polo Assn., Lexington
Kentucky Polo Assn., Louisville

LOUISIANA
Baton Rouge Polo Assn., Baton Rouge
Covington Polo Club, Covington
Folsom Polo Club, New Orleans
Palmetto Polo Club, Benton

MAINE
Down East Polo Club, South Harpswell

MARYLAND
Gone Away Farm, Poolesville
Potomac Polo Club, Rockville
Windsford Polo Club, Dickerson

MASSACHUSETTS
Cape Cod Polo Club, East Falmouth
Fox Lea Farm Polo Club, Rehoboth
Myopia Hunt Club, South Hamilton

MICHIGAN
Detroit Polo Club, Milford
Greater Grand Rapids Polo Club, Grand Rapids
Kentree Polo Club, Grand Rapids

MINNESOTA
Duluth Polo Club, Duluth
Twin City Polo Club, Maple Plain

MISSISSIPPI

Gulfport Polo Club, Gulfport
Jackson Polo Club, Jackson

MISSOURI

Kansas City Polo Club, Kansas City
St. Louis Country Club, Clayton

NEW HAMPSHIRE

Green Acres Polo Club, Dover

NEW MEXICO

Sante Fe Polo Grounds, Santa Fe
San Patricio Polo Club, San Patricio

NEW JERSEY

Briarwood Polo Club, Medford
Burnt Mills Polo Club, Bedminster
Far Hills Polo Club, Lebanon
Princeton Polo Club, Princeton
Ramapo Polo Club, Mahwah
Trump Valley Polo Club, Smithville

NEW YORK

Central New York Polo Club, Trumansburg
East Aurora Polo Club, East Aurora
Meadowbrook Polo Club, Jericho
Mendon Hill Polo Club, Rochester
Millbrook Polo Club, Millbrook
Owl Creek Polo Club, Scotia
Saratoga Polo Assn., Greenfield
Skaneateles Polo Club, Skaneateles
Unadilla Polo Club, Unadilla
Village Farms Polo Club, Gilbertsville
West Hills Polo Club, Huntington

NORTH CAROLINA

Charlotte Polo Club, Charlotte
Tanglewood Polo Club, Hillsborough

OHIO

Cincinnati Polo Club, Cincinnati
Cleveland Polo Club, Gates Mills

Columbus Farms, Columbus
Columbus Polo Club of Ohio, Columbus
Dayton Polo Club, Dayton
Mahoning Valley Polo Club, Canfield
Queen City Polo Club, Cincinnati

OKLAHOMA

Broad Acres Polo Club, Norman
Tulsa Polo & Hunt Club, Tulsa

OREGON

Eugene Polo Club, Eugene
Portland Polo Club, Portland

PENNSYLVANIA

Brandywine Polo Club, Toughkenamon
Chukker Valley Farms Polo Club, Gilbertsville
Darlington Polo Club, Darlington
Lancaster Polo Club, Rothsville
Mallet Hill Polo Club, Cochranville
Sewickley Polo Club, Sewickley
West Shore Polo Club, Mechanicsville

RHODE ISLAND

Newport Polo Assn., Portsmouth

SOUTH CAROLINA

Aiken Polo Club, Aiken
Camden Polo Club, Camden
Charleston Polo Club, Charleston
Hilton Head Polo Club, Bluffton
Midfield Polo Club, Camden
Rose Hill Plantation Polo Club, Bluffton

SOUTH DAKOTA

Pierre Polo Club, Pierre

TENNESSEE

Chattanooga Polo Assn., Chattanooga
Memphis Polo Assn., Memphis
Nashville Polo Assn., Nashville

TEXAS

Austin Polo Club, Austin
Houston Polo Assn., Houston
Lone Star Polo Club, Katy
Midland Polo Club, Midland
McFaddin Polo Club, McFaddin
Oak Hill Farms, Plano
Paso Del Norte Polo Assn., El Paso
Retama Polo Club, San Antonio
Rio Grande Polo Club, Kingsville
San Antonio Polo Club, San Antonio
San Saba Polo Club, San Saba
Spring Hill Farm Polo Club, Dallas
Wichita Falls Polo Club, Wichita Falls
Willow Bend Polo and Hunt Club, Plano

VERMONT

Quechee Polo Club, Quechee
Sugarbush Polo Club, Waitsfield

VIRGINIA

Bull Run Polo Club, Clifton
Casanova Polo Club, Casanova
Charlottesville Polo Club, Charlottesville
Farmington Hunt Club, Charlottesville
Middleburg Polo Club, Middleburg
Rappahannock Polo Club, Castleton

WASHINGTON

Bellingham Polo Club, Bellingham
Seattle Polo Club, Seattle
Spokane Polo Club, Spokane
Tacoma Polo Club, Tacoma

WISCONSIN

Joy Farm Polo Club, Milwaukee
Milwaukee Polo Club, Milwaukee
Olympia Polo Club, Milwaukee

WYOMING

Big Horn Polo Club, Big Horn
Cheyenne Polo Club, Cheyenne
Jackson Hole Polo Club, Jackson

CANADA

ALBERTA

Calgary Polo Club, Calgary
Grande Prairie Polo Club, Grande Prairie

BRITISH COLUMBIA

Vancouver Polo Club, Vancouver

ONTARIO

Toronto Polo Club, Toronto

MANITOBA

Springfield Polo Club, Dugald

QUEBEC

Montreal Polo Club, Hudson

Polo Goes to School

Arena polo is an established part of the athletic program at a growing number of colleges and universities, and at secondary schools as well. In many cases, alumni donate ponies and equipment to the programs, which are coached and supervised by noted players and trainers.

Intercollegiate and interscholastic games are held through the academic year, with year-end tournaments featuring top school teams. A number of these polo programs are listed below.

COLLEGES AND UNIVERSITIES

University of California–Davis, Davis, California
Cal Poly, San Luis Obispo, California
Colorado State University, Fort Collins, Colorado
University of Connecticut, Storrs, Connecticut
Cornell University, Ithaca, New York
Florida Atlantic, Palm Beach, Florida
Harvard University, Cambridge, Massachusetts
Los Angeles/Pierce College, Los Angeles, California
Pace University, Pleasantville, New York

Skidmore College, Saratoga Springs, New York
University of Southern California, Los Angeles, California
St. Andrews College, Aurora, Ontario, Canada
University of South Carolina, Camden, South Carolina
Stanford University, Stanford, California
Texas A & M, College Station, Texas
Texas Tech, Lubbock, Texas
Tulane University, New Orleans, Louisiana
University of Virginia, Charlottesville, Virginia
Xavier University, Cincinnati, Ohio
Yale University, New Haven, Connecticut

SECONDARY SCHOOLS

Cape Cod School, East Falmouth, Massachusetts
Culver Military Academy, Culver, Indiana
Garrison Forest School, Garrison, Maryland
Lawrenceville School, Lawrenceville, New Jersey
Moorpark Unified School District, Moorpark, California
Valley Forge Military Academy, Wayne, Pennsylvania

High-Goal Tournaments

High-goal, the phrase that polo enthusiasts use to describe the most important tournaments, refers less to the expected final scores than to the caliber of the participants, many of whom are among the world's highest-rated players. Unlike such sporting events as Major League baseball or NFL football, where teams have fixed schedules and starting lineups, exactly whom polo spectators will get to see in tournaments depends on which teams want to play, have been invited, or have qualified to participate. Similarly, specific lineups will often depend on who has been asked to play for a particular squad.

Despite its international aspect, polo is not a sport that is included in the Olympic Games. There is no indication that this omission will be corrected, although since host countries have the right to include sports of their own choosing, there is always that possibility.

Within the sport, however, are a number of tournaments that determine the world's best. The World Championships are held in August in the Normandy resort town of Deauville, France. Across the English Channel, the prestigious Coronation Cup is held in July, at Windsor

Great Park near London. Argentina, long a breeding ground of top players and ponies, hosts championships throughout the autumn months (remember that it's spring south of the equator). Closer to home, the Americas' Championship held in September in Greenwich, Connecticut, pits an all-star American squad against top players from South America.

Among other tournaments that traditionally attract top international teams are the ones that bear the names of Boehme, Rolex, Cartier, and Piaget (such corporate sponsorship, and the sizeable purses involved, are an element in their drawing power).

H. Kauffman & Sons polo team after a match at Ox Ridge Polo Club, Darien, Connecticut. (Left to right) Will Osborne, Lou Lopes, team sponsor Charles F. Kauffman, Charles Von Arenschildt, and Guy Gengris. (photo by Meredith Von Brock)

Several national titles are decided at the U.S. Open, the U.S. Handi-cap, the USPA President's Cup Finals, and the USPA National Arena Open.

Compiled from listings in equestrian magazines and other sports publications, the following schedule indicates the names and loca-tions of major U.S. high-goal tournaments (where no location is given, the tournament is held at a different site annually). For further information, including exact dates, refer to host facilities and/or schedules in polo and other equestrian magazines listed in Further Reading.

JANUARY

Boehme International Challenge Cup, Palm Beach Polo & Country Club, West Palm Beach, Florida

Sunshine League, Royal Palm Polo Club, Boca Raton, Florida

Cadillac National Polo League, Palm Beach Polo & Country Club, West Palm Beach, Florida

FEBRUARY

USPA Rolex Gold Cup, Palm Beach Polo & Country Club, West Palm Beach, Florida

The William Phillips Cup, Gulfstream Polo Club, Lake Worth, Florida

MARCH

International Challenge Cup (arena polo), Los Angeles Equestrian Center, Los Angeles, California

International Gold Cup, Royal Palm Polo Club, Boca Raton, Florida

Cartier International Open and Handicap, Palm Beach Polo & Country Club, West Palm Beach, Florida

APRIL

Piaget World Cup Championship, Palm Beach Polo & Country Club, West Palm Beach, Florida

American Polo League Spring season (through July), Los Angeles Equestrian Center, Los Angeles, California

The Alamo Cup, Freeman Coliseum, San Antonio, Texas

MAY

International Cup, Houston Polo Club, Houston, Texas

International All-Star Benefit, Potomac Polo Club, Poolesville, Maryland

North America Cup (through June)

JUNE

USPA Continental Cup (through July), Oak Brook, Illinois, and Milwaukee, Wisconsin

USPA Silver Cup, Willow Bend Polo Club, Plano, Texas

Greenwich Polo Club Sunday matches (through July), Greenwich, Connecticut

Pacific Gold Cup, Honolulu Polo Club, Honolulu, Hawaii

JULY

BMW East Coast Open, Myopia Polo Club, South Hamilton, Massachusetts

USPA America Cup, Santa Barbara Polo Club, Santa Barbara, California

Saratoga Polo Assn. (through August), Saratoga Springs, New York

Santa Barbara Trophy, Santa Barbara Polo Club, Santa Barbara, California

AUGUST

Calhoun Cup, Oak Brook Polo Club, Oak Brook, Illinois

International tournament play: a Cartier Coronation Cup match between England and Mexico. (Harold Roth/Equine Images)

Pacific Coast Open, Santa Barbara Polo Club, Santa Barbara, California
U.S. Cecil Smith, Oak Brook, Illinois
American Challenge, Newport Polo Assn., Portsmouth, Rhode Island
American Polo League Fall season (through December), Los Angeles Equestrian
    Center, Los Angeles, California
National Chairman's Cup

SEPTEMBER

U.S. Oak Brook Open and USPA Butler Handicap, Oak Brook Polo Club, Oak
    Brook, Illinois
The Americas' Championship, Greenwich Polo Club, Greenwich, Connecticut
U.S. Women's Handicap
National Inter-Circuit Tournament

OCTOBER

U.S. Open Championship
Rolex-USPA President's Cup Finals
U.S. Handicap

NOVEMBER

Village BMW Capital Cup (arena polo), Austin, Texas

DECEMBER

USPA National Arena Open

Polo Around the World

For further information about polo in these and other places, contact
the tourist boards of individual countries, or your travel agent.

   Other sources of information, once you have arrived at your desti-
nation, include the sports pages of local newspapers, equestrian magazines, and people at tack shops and stables.

MEXICO AND THE CARIBBEAN

Two clubs in Mexico are Las Anitas, in Chihuahua; and the Monterrey Polo Club, in the northeastern city of Monterrey.

   The most comprehensive polo resort facility in the Caribbean is
Casa de Campo, on the southern coast of the Dominican Republic.
Boasting two polo fields and 150 ponies, Casa de Campo offers instruction and opportunities to play at all levels, from beginner lessons
and stick and ball workouts, to frequent matches and high-goal tourna-

ments. There are also trail rides over the rolling coastland, while unmounted hours can be spent playing golf and tennis, or engaging in water sports such as swimming and snorkeling.

Vacationers to the Dominican Republic can also watch matches at the Romana Polo Club in La Romana.

The Chukka Cove Polo Club in Ocho Rios, Jamaica, hosts high-goal tournaments through the winter months.

EUROPE

England, the historical home of modern polo, remains a center of activity. The Warwickshire Cup takes place in Cirencester in June. Windsor Great Park is the site of the Queen's Cup in early June, and the Coronation Cup and Silver Jubilee Cup in late July. Also in July is high-goal polo at Cowdray Park.

Polo matches in the Republic of Ireland can be found during the summer months at Dublin's Phoenix Park.

France's polo activities include the Gold Cup World Championship held in August in the Normandy resort town of Deauville.

In Spain, Madrid is the venue of the Copa Real Club de la Hierro, a 10-day tournament in June. The Gold Cup takes place in mid-August in Sotogrande.

SOUTH AMERICA

Visitors to Argentina will be treated to some of the world's finest, and most enthusiastically received, polo at the Copa Repubica Argentina in Palermo. The Argentine Open Championship, also held in Palermo, takes place throughout November. Earlier in autumn is the Indios Tortugas Open, a 3-week tournament beginning in mid-September in Tortugas.

PHILIPPINES

There is polo activity at the Fort Stotsenburg Polo Club at Clark Air Force Base, and at the Manila Polo Club.

AUSTRALIA

Polo "down under" includes the Australasian Gold Cup in January in Perth, and the Sydney Royal Easter Show and Andronicus Coffee Easter International, both held in Sydney in April.

Polo Clinics

Taking part in a clinic, the term for intensive group instruction, is a highly effective way to learn to play or for more advanced players to improve their skills. The following sampling of domestic and foreign clinics range in prices from $400 to $1500 (use of ponies and equipment is included in the fees).

Major Hugh Dawnay, a well-regarded instructor, conducts his 6-day Polo Vision clinics at the Palm Beach Polo & Country Club in West Palm Beach, Florida, from January through April. Major Dawnay also holds a 3-week clinic in May at the Greenwich Polo Club in Greenwich, Connecticut.

Rege Ludwig holds 1-week beginner and intermediate-level clinics from late May to late June at the University of Virginia, in Charlottesville, Virginia.

Ludwig and Corky Linfoot lead weekend-long beginner clinics in April and November at the Eldorado Polo Club in Palm Desert, California.

Experienced players will be interested in twice-weekly clinics that run from May to July at the Willow Bend Polo and Hunt Club in Plano, Texas.

Travelers to the Caribbean will find clinics at both the Chukka Cove Polo Club in Ocho Rios, Jamaica, and at Casa de Campo in the Dominican Republic.

Near Buenos Aires, Argentina, are two world-famous teaching and playing establishments. La Martina Polo Club features instruction under coach Horacio Heguy. The Palermo Polo Club is the home base of Gonzalo Pieres, considered by many to be the foremost contemporary player in the world. When he is at home, Pieres joins instructor Tolo Ocampo in giving lessons.

Located at the Guards Polo Club at Windsor, England, the Rangitiki Polo School offers clinics by Peter Grace.

Further Reading

Books

Yearbook of the United States Polo Association (annually): Anyone interested in playing the sport should own, and make use of, this annual compendium. Included are outdoor and arena Rules of Play, player handicaps, and the names and addresses of member clubs and schools. (Available in hardcover or spiral-bound paperback from the USPA, 120 North Mill Street, Lexington, Kentucky, 40507.)

Polo Vision by Hugh Dawnay (J. A. Allen, 1986): Major Dawnay, the noted instructor and clinician, stresses more than fundamentals in this excellent book. He offers exercises and strategies based on an integrated and logical progression toward a comprehensive understanding of the game.

An Introduction to Polo by "Marco" (J. A. Allen, 1976): A British classic, the book offers basic instruction in hitting, team play, and specimen attacks.

Practical Polo by W. G. Vickers (J. A. Allen, 1974): Another British manual, this one also treats the basics of individual strokes and team play.

The Polo Handbook, Volumes One (1977) and Two (1984): Compiled from articles that first appeared in *Polo* magazine, these useful anthologies cover a wide range of subjects, from strategies and umpiring, to training ponies and mallet repair.

Periodicals

Polo (eight issues a year): The sport's "magazine of record," *Polo* features tournament coverage, instructional articles, reports of new products and services, and other items of interest.

The Chronicle of the Horse (weekly): This general-interest English-style equestrian magazine periodically includes articles on American outdoor and arena polo.

Campo De Polo (semiannually): An Argentine magazine (in Spanish) that covers items of interest in South America, as well as the rest of the polo world.

Index